# Romance Unbound Publishing

**Presents**

# The Master

Claire Thompson

Edited by
Donna Fisk
Jae Ashley

Cover Art by Kelly Shorten
Fine Line Edit by Kevin Gherlone

Print ISBN 978-1484850459
Copyright 2013 Claire Thompson
All rights reserved

# Chapter 1

Whips brushed bare skin, the cracking sound punctuated by breathy sighs and moans. Jaime Heller, staring down into her glass as she sat hunched on the barstool, barely noticed. She wasn't in the right headspace for BDSM play tonight. She should have gone straight home after work instead of coming to the club.

Her briefcase, bulging with loan documents and financial reports, was crammed into a locker in the women's changing room, along with her corporate outfit of navy blue jacket, crisp white blouse, tailored skirt, annoying pantyhose and sensible pumps. She'd changed into her favorite black silk blouse and leather pants upon arriving at the club, and brought her gear bag with her to the juice bar, but her heart just wasn't in it tonight.

A tap on her shoulder made her lift her head. There stood Ryan Holcombe, model-perfect, a broad smile on his handsome face. Jaime knew what he wanted, even before he held up his favorite single tail, his expression puppy-dog eager. Before he could speak, she shook her head. "Not tonight, Ryan. Sorry."

As he melted back into the crowd, Betsy appeared beside Jaime. Betsy Hanover was the owner of Betsy's

Bondage Bar, a trendy BDSM club located in New York City's Greenwich Village. Though Betsy was almost old enough to be Jaime's mother, Jaime considered her a friend.

"We need to talk," Betsy informed her in her no-nonsense tone.

"About?"

"Let's go sit in a booth." Without waiting to see if Jaime followed, Betsy headed toward a private booth at the back of the room.

When Jaime slid onto the padded leather seat across from her, Betsy said, "I saw you send Ryan away just now. What's going on with you, Jaime?"

Jaime shrugged. "I don't know. Rough day at the office. The usual shit, I guess."

"It's more than that," Betsy asserted. "I've watched you over the past few months. It's almost like you're just going through the motions. When you scene with these sub boys, I can't help but get the feeling you're meeting their needs, not yours. Have you ever considered playing the other side of the fence?"

Jaime looked up at her friend, incredulous. "What? Are you out of your mind? I'm a Domme. You know that."

"I know you walk the walk and carry the whip, but it's not always so clear cut, my dear. Have you ever let yourself be truly vulnerable? Have you ever experienced what you give your sub boys? Even if you're primarily dominant, completely surrendering your will to another person can be intensely powerful. If nothing else, it can be an incredible stress release."

Jaime snorted. "No way, Betsy. I'm not hardwired that way." Even as she said this, Jaime felt a sudden frisson of—what? Fear? Anticipation? Desire?—move along her spine.

"I wouldn't be so quick to dismiss it out of hand, Jaime. I have some insight into you, you know."

"Oh stop," Jaime said, not liking this line of conversation. "It's just work. That's the problem. It's always the problem. I have this loan presentation on Monday and I can't even stand to open my briefcase, much less crunch the stupid numbers. I wake up in the middle of the night in a cold sweat, bursting from a nightmare like I'm crashing through a pane of glass. It's always the same—me standing naked in front of the loan committee with no idea about the deal I'm supposed to be presenting.

"When my alarm goes off at the crack of fucking dawn so I can make the commute into a city I could never afford to actually live in, my head is already pounding. Before I even get to work, Aiken's sent me seven emails and four text messages informing me of the massive pile of shit he's already dumped on my desk, berating me for the latest string of fuckups he claims I've made or clients who need their hands held, and threatening me about how the bank's tightening its belt and a pink slip isn't just something I wear under my skirt."

"He actually said that?" Betsy laughed, shaking her head.

"He did. And that's the sanitized version. Bob Aiken is worse than one of those movies about the boss from hell." Jaime sighed. "I hate my fucking boss. I hate my fucking job. I hate my fucking life." The words came out with more vehemence than Jaime had intended, but she knew they were true. And this cold, hard reality hit her like a fist in the gut.

Taking a deep breath, Jaime looked down at the table. Tears were burning behind her eyelids and she blinked them angrily away. Betsy put a hand on her arm. "Jaime, honey. Look at me." Jaime looked into the kind face of her friend and found more tears threatening. "Life is too short to keep on the way you're going, babe. You need to make a change."

"Tell me about it," Jaime retorted. "I just found out I make ten thousand less than the jerk who sits next to me and has been at the bank for two years less than I have, but he has this big advantage, at least in Aiken's eyes—he has a dick."

"We need to get your boss in here. A few hours spent bound in the stocks with a large dildo shoved up his ass might adjust the old boy's mindset." Betsy flashed an evil grin.

Jaime groaned. "Please, the thought of him naked is enough to make me puke. Though it would be good for him to indulge in a little role reversal. We could dress him up in a corset and heels, put him in a wig with full makeup and make him bend over for twenty licks with the paddle."

The image of Bob Aiken, with his wobbly jowls, small, piggy eyes and pug nose heavily made up with pancake foundation, rouge, lipstick and false eyelashes made Jaime shudder in amused horror. "Do you know what he actually had the audacity to say the other day, after reaming me for like twenty minutes in front of the other guys, 'If you can't take the heat, *Ms.* Heller'—he says *Ms.* like it's a curse word—'get back in the kitchen where you belong.'"

Betsy's mouth fell open. "Oh, my god. He actually *said* that? Aren't there laws against that kind of thing?"

"If I tried to do anything about it, I'd be told I'm not a *team player*. They're big on team players at the bank. We're all part of a team. Let's get out there, team! Let's hump it, people! Let's go, go, go!" Jaime felt her blood pressure rising and took a deep breath, willing herself to relax. "When he says that, all I want to do is go, go, go, right out the door and never come back."

"Why don't you?"

"Huh? Why don't I what?"

"Why don't you go and never come back?"

Jaime stared at Betsy, confused. "You mean leave? Quit the job at the bank? Just like that?"

Betsy nodded. "Just like that."

Jaime smiled ruefully. "No offense, Bets, but not everyone has the options you do. Especially in this economy." Betsy had family money, as she called it, and had never had to scrabble to make ends meet like most of the rest of humanity.

"Everyone has a choice, Jaime. You're what, twenty-six?"

"Almost twenty-seven."

"That's old enough to know what you want, and what you don't want. That's old enough to say, I'm *done* being miserable. If I hate my fucking boss and I hate my fucking job and I hate my fucking life, I'm going to fucking *do* something about it."

Jaime grinned in spite of herself. "Yeah, like what? Like give Aiken the proverbial third finger salute, climb in my car and just start driving? Don't think I haven't thought about it."

"Yes!" Betsy said, hitting the table between them with her fist. "That's it exactly."

~*~

Jaime left the club soon after, taking the train back to her New Jersey suburb and hurling her stuff into the back seat of her car once she got into the station. She parked as close as she could to her apartment building, slung her duffel bag and purse over her shoulder and grabbed her overloaded briefcase. At the building, she entered the code on the keypad to unlock the thick glass doors at the entrance.

While struggling to open her mailbox, she dropped her briefcase and it sprang open, spilling piles of papers and files onto the floor of the foyer. With a groan, Jaime squatted and collected the mess, shoving it back into the briefcase, along with the junk mail from her mailbox.

The ancient elevator lurched as it lifted her to her third floor apartment. There was a thick white envelope taped across her door. Curious and a little alarmed, Jaime pulled the envelope free and unlocked her door, entering the apartment and dropping her briefcase and duffel just inside.

Collapsing onto the sofa, she tore open the letter, which was addressed to "The Tenant in Apartment 3B."

"What the fuck," she breathed, as she scanned the official looking letter from a law firm that purported to represent the real estate holdings of the building owners. It was an eviction letter, basically. Well, not if she could come up with a ridiculous sum of money by the end of the month. The building, it seemed, was being turned into a co-op. The owners of the building were magnanimously allowing her the option of buying this cramped, overpriced dump of an apartment, or she could get her stuff out by the end of the month, per the terms of the lease, which allow for such a contingency, blah, blah, blah…

With a sigh, Jaime hoisted herself from the sofa and went over to her laptop, waking it up. As it booted to life, she heard the ping of incoming mail on the email server from the bank. Knowing in advance she would regret it, she couldn't resist her morbid impulse to check the mail.

There was an email was from Dennis O'Brien, the one guy on her team she could tolerate. The subject read: *Collateral Analysis Update*, which was their code header to throw nosy techies in the bank's IT department off the track. It was established lore at the bank that the techies had the ability, if not the authority, to read anyone's email, and even if it wasn't true, why take the chance.

Jaime opened the email.

*I just got word from Brenda over in the EVP's office. Our overall profit numbers this month weren't high enough for the Talking Heads in corporate. Aiken's on the warpath. He's going to call a meeting right after loan committee and tear us all a new one. Oh boy, can't wait. I hear you have a shit deal to present. Better figure out how*

*to fudge those numbers. Have a great weekend. Ha ha.
Dennis*

Walking dejectedly into the bedroom, Jaime took off her clothing, intending to pull on her sleep T-shirt and get ready for bed. Instead she found herself dressing again, this time in a knit shirt and her favorite jeans. She pulled on socks and her hiking boots, adrenaline kicking in as she realized what she was going to do.

She dragged out her large suitcase from under the bed. Placing it open on the mattress, she began to empty her closet and drawers into the case — no work clothes, just her comfy weekend things, along with her BDSM outfits and gear. She added her jewelry, her Kindle, her makeup bag and toiletries and her favorite pillow.

Pulling the wheeled suitcase into the living room, she retrieved her computer bag from the hall closet and packed her laptop, phone charger and the files and important personal papers from her desk.

At the last minute she grabbed the briefcase. She'd ship the entire contents to Aiken when she got around to it. He could sort it out.

She glanced around the apartment, thinking how little she'd accumulated, and how little what she did have mattered. Let the landlords have it. She didn't want any of it. She'd start fresh. And she'd start now.

Sitting at the desk, she pulled out a red marker from the drawer and wrote across the eviction letter:

*Thanks, but no thanks*, and scrawled her signature beneath it. She tucked it into the stamped, self addressed envelope the law firm had so thoughtfully provided, and dropped the letter into the mail chute while she waited for the elevator to take her down and out into the wide, open night, which was suddenly filled with possibility.

~*~

It was three o'clock the next day when Jaime pulled into another in a series of rest stops. Propelled forward by nervous energy, she'd been driving nearly nonstop since the night before, stopping only to grab a few hours sleep along the way.

Taking her cell phone from the car charger, she called Betsy. "I did it," she announced.

"Hello to you too, Jaime." Betsy laughed. "You did what?"

"I left. Packed my bags and hit the road."

There was a brief pause, and then, "You did? Really? Where are you?"

"Just outside of Chicago. I have no idea where I'm going, but it feels great."

"You quit your job? What about your apartment?"

"I haven't officially quit yet. When I got home last night, it turns out they want to evict me anyway. I took that as a sign from the universe. It's time to get the hell out of Dodge." Jaime laughed.

"That's great!" Betsy enthused. "You sound like your old self, too. I haven't heard you laugh in ages. So what's the plan?"

"No plan. I'm just driving. I have no idea where I'm going. Crazy, right?"

"Not so crazy. I've got an idea, if you're interested. You're on I-80?"

"Yep."

"Just stay on it another couple thousand miles," Betsy said with a laugh. "Seriously, though. I have friends in San Francisco. They own a really cool club out there. You could get a job there. Start fresh. If you needed some money I could—"

"That's okay," Jaime interrupted. "I've got some savings. I'm good."

"Okay. Well, know I'm here if you ever need me. Meanwhile, here are the details."

~*~

Jaime lifted her hips and pushed her hand into her jeans pocket. She extracted the piece of paper, now crumpled, and smoothed it open on her thigh. Behind her somebody honked their horn, and she glanced up at the light, which had turned green.

"I need coffee," she said aloud, though she was alone. Her eyes burned and her butt was asleep. Her car clock, still on New York time, read 8:22 am. The sun was just rising, or more accurately, trying to push its way through the San Franciscan fog on that Monday morning.

Jaime pulled into a donut shop and climbed stiffly out of the car. As she stood, the piece of paper fell to the asphalt of the parking lot. She bent to pick it up.

*The Bondage Wheel – 225 Columbus Avenue. Ask for Gene.*

Folding it back into her pocket, Jaime entered the shop and sat down at the counter. The woman behind the counter was placing donuts onto angled racks that lined the back wall. She was wearing a pink uniform with a white apron. She didn't seem to realize Jaime was there.

Jaime clinked her keys onto the counter to get her attention. After she'd sorted the last of the donuts, the woman finally turned and faced Jaime. A plastic name badge was pinned over her left breast that read, *I'm Mary*, and just below that, *How May I Help You?*

"Morning," Mary said in a dull voice. Her mouth was drawn down at the corners in a frown and she looked haggard. "What can I get you?"

"Morning," Jaime replied. "I'll have a medium coffee with cream and two sugars and," she paused, looking over the various donut offerings, "I'll have one of those maple frosteds and a glazed."

"Here or to go?"

"Here. Uh, do you have a restroom?"

The woman jerked her head to the left. "Back there."

Jaime went into the bathroom, peed and washed her face and hands. She stared at herself in the mirror and ran her fingers through her short hair, which was standing up in unruly tufts around a face that looked tired, dark smudges under her eyes.

Just the same, Jaime flashed herself an incredulous smile. "I did it," she whispered triumphantly to the mirror image. "I'm in San Francisco! I'm free!"

She patted the piece of paper in her pocket and returned to her stool, sliding up onto it and taking a sip of strong, hot coffee. She took a big bite of the maple frosted donut and washed it down with another sip of coffee. Two people came into the shop while she was eating, ordered donuts and coffee to go and left.

When she got Mary's attention again, Jaime said, "Is there a cheap motel somewhere around here?"

Mary shook her head. "Nothing's cheap in San Francisco. But there's a Motel 8 a couple of blocks over. Where you from?"

"New Jersey."

"What brings you all this way?"

"I ran away."

Mary looked her up and down, her expression skeptical. "Excuse me, but you look a little too old to be running away from home. No offense."

Jaime laughed. "None taken. I'm twenty-seven today, in fact. It's my birthday."

"Well, happy birthday." Mary smiled a genuine smile, making her look suddenly younger than Jaime had initially thought.

"Thanks." Jaime smiled back.

"Here." Mary turned to grab a donut covered with pink frosting and colored sprinkles. "A birthday donut."

Jaime smiled at the kind gesture, though she would have rather had another maple frosted. "Thanks," she said, taking the donut.

"So you ran away, huh," Mary persisted. "What from?"

Jaime shrugged. "Maybe run away isn't the right term. Escape is more like it."

She leaned forward on her elbows on the counter, still not quite believing herself what she'd done. "Ever get to the point you just want to get in the car and keep on driving?"

Mary offered a hard, angry smile. "Just about every day," she said. "Look where I'm working." She waved her hand around the small coffee shop. "I spent twenty-two years with the same company. Then they merged with another company and suddenly I became redundant. That's the word they used. Redundant. They gave me two weeks pay and let me go. Just like that. Out the door."

"That sucks," Jaime said sympathetically.

"Yeah," Mary agreed. She refilled Jaime's cup. "So what about you? You redundant too?"

"Nope. I'm homeless and jobless, but redundant? Never." She laughed, feeling absurdly light. A text buzzed on her phone and Jaime looked at it. It was from her boss.

*I need you in early this morning. Complications with the loan packet.*

Jaime's gut clenched reflexively, until her brain reminded it she was *free*!

She texted back: *So sorry. I won't be in today.*

Aiken responded: *I don't care if you're puking your guts out. If you don't get your ass here pronto, you're fired.*

Jaime's thumbs actually shook as she typed back: *Too late. I quit.*

Then a grin spread over her face and she laughed out loud as she dropped her phone into her purse.

"You sure seem happy for someone with no job or place to live," Mary remarked, as she topped off Jaime's coffee.

"I just told my boss, I mean my ex-boss, that I quit."

"No kidding. That must feel good."

"Feels great," Jaime agreed. She took a bite of the pink-frosted donut, surprised by how good it was.

"Sounds like your job must have been pretty bad, huh?"

"The job itself wasn't so bad, I guess, if you like getting paid less than your male coworkers even though you have more experience and do a better job. And if you like making cold calls to companies, trying to get them to borrow money from you that they don't need, because the ones that need it can't qualify for a loan. And if you enjoy sitting in endless, mind numbing meetings with a bullying boss who pits the loan officers against each other and motivates through fear and aggression. Oh, and if you don't mind when he dumps a big stack of files on your desk on a Friday at six o'clock and says you better be ready to present the loan package first thing Monday morning for a company that has no business borrowing funds, but the owner is a special pal of the boss, and if the deal doesn't get approved he'll fire your ass in a New York minute."

Even as she rambled on, Jaime knew she was saying too much, and to a perfect stranger at that. It must be the sleep deprivation of the past days, along with the giddiness at her new situation. "Pardon the rant." She smiled sheepishly at Mary. "You must think I'm nuts."

"Not at all," Mary assured her, her tone earnest. "It's like some kind of movie. Everyone's fantasy — to just get in the car and keep on going. Is that what happened?"

Jaime nodded, amazed anew at what she'd done. "Pretty much. I'm supposed to be at that meeting right now, selling the loan committee on a bad piece of business. I've been at that job for six years and I still haven't paid off all my student loans for a degree in finance I never should have gotten in the first place. I guess it was the eviction notice taped to my apartment door when I got home from work that put me over the edge. They're turning my apartment complex into a co-op apparently." She shrugged, still grinning. "I just packed up the stuff I care about and left the rest. Let them deal with it."

Mary was grinning now too. "You go, girl!" she enthused.

"I'm Jaime, by the way." Jaime extended her hand across the bar.

"Pleased to meet you. I'm Mary." Mary touched the plastic nametag on her uniform. "By the way, I think they're hiring at the gas station next door. I could put in a good word for you."

Jaime smiled at the stranger's kindness. "That's really nice of you, thanks. I'll be all right for a while, but I do need to find someplace to stay."

Mary reached into her apron pocket and took out a pad of paper. "I've got a cousin who has a garage apartment over in North Beach. She just lost her tenant and is going to be putting a want ad in the papers. You'd need to have two months' rent and the place is pretty tiny, but—"

"Sounds perfect," Jaime interjected.

"Okay." Mary tore a piece of paper from the pad and handed it to Jaime, along with a pen. "Write your phone number here, and I'll have her give you a call."

~*~

Jaime drove past the club twice looking for a parking place. It was bad enough parallel parking on the busy street, but the fact it was on a steep hill did nothing to help matters. It was a few minutes before seven, the sun not yet set on a clear June evening. Gene had told her to come by at seven for an interview. She could hardly believe her luck—at this rate she would have a job and a place to live within days of arriving in a new city! It must be fate, she decided with a satisfied grin.

Before checking in at the motel, Jaime had placed a call to the human resources department at the bank to let them know she would no longer be working there, and had been told her last check would be deposited into her account, along with whatever vacation pay and accrued sick time she was owed. Meanwhile she had $5,400 in her checking account, enough to last her a little while, even if she didn't find a job right way.

She'd spent the afternoon crashed out on an overly-soft mattress at the Motel 8 near the donut shop, sleeping for nearly ten hours before waking to take a shower and head out in search of food. She checked her phone in case Mary's cousin had called, but the only phone messages were from Aiken. Jaime erased them all without listening to them, her spirit lightening each time she hit the delete button.

Now Jaime climbed out of her car and tugged at the hem of her slinky black dress. There was a cool, damp breeze and she shivered, pulling her silk shawl around her shoulders as she walked carefully in her heels to the front door of the club. There were no windows and no real indication of what was behind the large red door, but that was typical for this sort of club, where discretion was paramount.

Still, for a moment she worried she was at the wrong place. Then she noticed the small brass placard over an intercom box, with the words: *The Bondage Wheel – Members Only*. Licking her lips and taking a deep breath, Jaime pushed the buzzer on the intercom and stepped back, waiting.

After a few beats, a voice came through the speaker. "May I help you?"

"Yes. I'm Jaime Heller. I called earlier?"

"Yeah, okay. Hold on. I'll be right there."

After another few moments, there was the sound of a bolt being pulled back on the other side of the door, and then it swung inward. A big man of about forty with a thick mop of curly blond hair and kind eyes smiled down at her as he extended a beefy hand.

"Jaime. It's a pleasure to meet you. I'm Gene Mueller."

Her small hand was swallowed in his huge one. Letting her go, he stepped back. "Come on back to my office and we'll talk."

Jaime followed, thinking as she often did that it wasn't what you did so much as who you knew when it came to things like housing and jobs. Thank goodness for Betsy!

The front room of the club had a fully stocked bar flanked by high leather stools. Gene led her through the barroom to the main dungeon play area, which included all the usual BDSM equipment and toys any well-stocked BDSM club contained. In addition to the crosses, whipping posts, stocks and displays of whips, paddles, canes and floggers, a huge bondage wheel had been mounted on the back wall. It was completely covered in black leather, save for a red leather X in the center of the circle. Restraining cuffs were placed at intervals along the red X.

"Wow," Jaime enthused. "That's fantastic."

Gene smiled proudly. "Isn't it great? We had it built special for the club when we opened." He moved toward the wheel and gave it a spin. Though Jaime would have liked a turn with it herself, Gene was already continuing on through an opening that led to a series of doors. Jaime followed him into a large office with windows that looked out on a parking lot.

"Betsy told me you might be calling," Gene said as he settled behind a glass-topped desk and waved Jaime into a chair. "She says you're into the scene. Always happy to meet a fellow enthusiast."

Jaime nodded. "Yeah. I've been active in the scene for about five years now. I definitely know my way around a whip. If you need a pro Dominatrix, I'm sure I could learn whatever's needed to fill the position."

Gene shook his head. "My partner, Donovan, is our Master in residence. The Master, as folks call him, has made quite a name for himself in the fetish and leather community. He does a stage show just about every night to standing room only."

He leaned forward. "We do, however, have need of a waitress and someone to help the bartender. I like to hire within the community when I can and you're a nice piece of eye candy, if you don't mind my saying. You have any experience waitressing?" He looked Jaime up and down. Normally she would have bristled at this, but she understood she was being interviewed for a job at a sex club, and she had dressed the part, too.

Jaime nodded. "I put myself through college working tables."

"Excellent. The club opens at nine," Gene said. He leaned back in his chair, putting his hands behind his head. "You would need to be here at eight to help with set up. There's a small parking lot around back you can use." He waved a hand toward the window. "We're open Tuesday through Saturday nights. It's the usual lousy waitstaff pay but you get to keep all your tips. Interested?"

"I sure am," Jaime said. "I'm curious though, alcohol at a BDSM club?"

"It's never been a problem for us. Not everyone who comes here comes to scene. A lot of them just come to gawk." Gene grinned and leaned back in his chair, his eyes still roving over Jaime. "As you saw, the dungeon is fully equipped and there's space for folks to do their own scenes. The serious players know better than to drink and play, and we keep a bouncer on the premises just to make sure nobody does anything stupid. That's Tommy. He also functions as an extra if folks need a little help in their scenes."

Gene leaned forward again, resting his elbows on his desk. "Your timing couldn't be better. The last girl gave notice this past week due to family problems and we've been having a hell of a time without her. You can start tomorrow if you want. We provide the uniform, which is in keeping with the spirit of the club. What are you, a size six?"

Jaime nodded, impressed he had guessed correctly. "What's this uniform made of? I'm not big on those PVC cat suits, I can tell you right now."

Gene laughed. "No, no cat suits for the servers. It's more like a French maid outfit, polyester with a little spandex thrown in, though the bustier is leather. Here. I'll show you."

He stood, moving toward a large wardrobe in the corner of the office. Pulling open the double doors, he rifled through the rack and pulled out an outfit that consisted of a very low cut black dress with spaghetti straps, a white frilled apron and a soft black leather bustier with satin ties that laced up the front. "The bustier goes right over the dress. No bra needed. Try it on before you go. The staff changing room is right next to my office. You can keep your stuff there while you're at work. We keep the uniforms here and they're professionally cleaned every week."

A thrill of excitement leaped through Jaime's gut. Here she was her first night in San Francisco and she already had a job! So, the money was shit—she liked that Gene was upfront about that—but she also knew from her waitressing days that the tips could be pretty substantial. True, she didn't yet have anywhere to live, but hopefully Mary's cousin would be calling shortly and she'd get the garage apartment.

Had she really managed to leave the rat race of corporate America four thousand miles behind her? Was she done with always doing exactly what was expected of her? Was she finished taking the safe but deadly dull route?

Shit, yeah! Betsy was right—it was time to follow her dreams.

Now if she could just figure out what those dreams were, she thought wryly.

"So what do you say? You want the job?"

Jaime leaned over the desk and extended her hand. "I sure do."

# Chapter 2

It was her first night at the club, and she'd been working nonstop from the minute she had arrived at eight, helping set up the bar, and then serving customers drinks as well as snacks from the limited menu. She had forgotten just how physical waitressing was. It was nearly eleven and her feet were killing her.

*Note to self: buy comfortable shoes first thing in the morning.*

Gene came by the bar just as Jaime took a tray of beer bottles and glasses from the bartender. "You're doing good, kid. Once you finish that order take a ten minute break. I'll cover for you." He waved toward the dungeon. "Check out the action if you want. The Master is gearing up for his first show of the night."

"Thanks."

A glass of ice water in her hand, Jaime slipped in among a crowd of leather- and latex-clad customers, some of them engaged in their own scenes at various play stations around the dungeon, but most of them gathered in a semicircle around the bondage wheel.

Jaime moved closer, standing on the edge of the crowd. The Master was turned away from her as he strapped the woman onto the wheel. His dark hair was glossy, his broad, muscular back rippling beneath the soft black leather of his vest. A tattoo of three intertwined snakes curled around the bulging biceps of his left arm.

Though Jaime couldn't see his face, something about the man tugged at her senses, jump starting her heart into a hard, steady beat. *Not my type*, her brain attempted to inform her, but her body wasn't listening.

A spotlight flicked directly over the bondage wheel, drawing Jaime's eye reluctantly from the Master to the bound woman at its center. The woman had a red satin sleep mask over her eyes. Her blond hair hung to her shoulders. Her skin was deeply tanned, her lips painted a vivid red. Jaime guessed from the softening at her jaw line and the slight sag of her breasts that she was somewhere in her forties, though she appeared toned and athletic. She was naked, save for shiny red high heels and a pair of black leather panties held in place with thin silver chains over her hips. Her wrists, waist, thighs and ankles were locked into the thick black leather cuffs that were strategically placed along the X.

The Master reached out his hand, on which he wore fingerless black leather riding gloves, and stroked the woman's cheek. "Are you ready to suffer for me, slave?"

Jaime still couldn't see the Master's face, but something in the timbre of his rich, deep voice made the hairs on the back of her neck stand up, and she found herself, absurdly, wanting to answer for the woman.

*Yes.*

The room felt suddenly too close, the press of people around her sucking the air from her lungs. Jaime lifted the glass of ice water to her temple and closed her eyes.

"Yes, Master," the woman answered in a husky, raspy voice Jaime associated with a heavy smoker.

The Master turned at last to face the crowd that had assembled around the bondage wheel. He had piercing blue eyes beneath thick, straight brows. His nose was prominent and slightly crooked, his jaw square and covered with a few days' stubble. Jaime guessed him to be in his late twenties or early thirties. Though he wasn't precisely handsome — his eyes set a little too close together, his nose a little too large — he was compelling in a way that made it impossible for Jaime to take her eyes off him.

She could feel the power radiating from him like an aura. He wasn't a player, but the real thing. Which was too bad, since she had already placed him on the bondage wheel in her mind's eye, stripped of the leather trappings, his naked, muscular body spread taut along the X in its center.

The Master addressed the group gathered before him. "Tonight this slave will endure a full body caning while being stimulated with a butterfly vibrator. I need a volunteer—someone familiar with rotating the wheel."

Several men stepped forward, calling out in their eagerness to participate.

"Fred." The Master pointed to a short, heavyset man, who came quickly forward and stepped to the opposite side of the wheel from the Master. "Turn her slowly once I begin the caning." Fred placed his hand on the edge of the wheel, his eyes moving hungrily over the restrained and blindfolded woman.

The Master pressed a button on a small remote Jaime now saw he held in his hand and turned to address the audience. "Beth's stated goal is to remain silent during the erotic torture, without the aid of a gag. I've worked with Beth before, and she has a high pain threshold but is easily stimulated."

Selecting a short, thin cane from a rack containing dozens of canes, whips, paddles and floggers, the Master began to tap the tops of Beth's breasts, leaving small horizontal red marks just above her erect brown nipples. Save for the humming sound of the vibrator tucked into the woman's leather panties, the dungeon had grown silent, as if the crowd held its collective breath.

Though there was still the sound of conversation and clinking glass from the bar in the room beyond, Jaime focused on the swish and tap of the cane held in the Master's easy, confident grip. Fred turned the wheel slowly. When Beth was upside down, the tips of her hair sweeping the stage, the Master ordered, "Stop. Keep her there."

He focused the cane on Beth's upper thighs, his strokes firmer now, the lines left behind on her skin longer and darker. Her lips had parted and Jaime noted that her hands were clenched into fists above the leather cuffs, but so far she'd managed to remain quiet. A fiery stroke across her left nipple caused the woman to hiss in a sudden intake of breath, and droplets of sweat were visible on her chest and upper lip.

The Master nodded toward Fred, who again began to spin the wheel in a slow, easy motion while the woman shuddered and twitched in her bonds, her mouth opened in a perfect O.

Jaime wasn't usually much for public play. Her scenes at Betsy's place were generally prearranged with one of the sub boy regulars there. She liked to have them ready and waiting in a private play space on their knees, forehead on the ground when she arrived. On the rare occasions she did watch someone else's scene, it would be a Dominatrix and her boy — Jaime had no interest in watching women submit to men.

So why was she unable to tear her eyes away from the scene before her?

When Beth began to tremble, her hips gyrating in time to the vibrating butterfly between her legs, the Master whipped her harder, each stroke of the cane leaving a ridged welt in its wake on the woman's breasts, belly and thighs. Small guttural sounds came from her throat, keeping time with the whoosh and cut of the cane.

Jaime pressed her legs together to still her throbbing clit. She was clutching the water glass in both hands against her chest, her teeth worrying her lower lip, her nipples hard against the leather bustier.

She gave a small, involuntary gasp when someone's hand rested heavily on her shoulder. Jerking back toward Gene, she accidently sloshed the water in her glass, causing it to spill in an icy splatter between her breasts.

Gene's lips lifted in a half smile, his eyebrow cocking. He bent close, his mouth near her ear. "You're needed at the bar," he said softly. "A party of six just came in. Break's over."

~*~

Donovan took a deep pull on the cold beer and set the bottle on the bar. It had been a long night, with two public scenes and three private ones, and he was wiped out. The club would be closing in a few minutes, and he swiveled on the barstool to watch the new girl as she collected empty bottles and glasses and exchanged a few words with some of the last lingering customers.

She was a hot little number, with short reddish hair streaked with gold, and large soft green eyes the color of sage. She wasn't tall, even in those fuck-me high heels she was wearing, but she was every bit a woman, curving in all the right places, her breasts offered up in her black bustier like luscious round peaches.

Gene slid onto the stool beside Donovan. "A good night for a Tuesday," he said, a cash resister tape in his hand. Gene was the money man of the partnership, which suited Donovan, who much preferred providing the entertainment. Together they made a good team, and the club, now entering its fifth year, was firmly established and finally turning a nice profit, despite the insanely high rent of the upscale San Franciscan neighborhood.

Annette, who was wiping down the bar, leaned over it to kiss the top of Gene's head. She had dark, curly hair and snapping black eyes. Gene twisted back and reached for her, kissing her mouth. Donovan smiled as he watched them. Though you wouldn't know it from looking at them, Annette called the shots in the relationship, which was a 24/7 Mistress/slave love match that Donovan almost envied.

He'd had plenty of sub girls in his day, some of them even live-in lovers, but he'd never experienced the kind of intense devotion Gene and Annette seemed to share. Not that he really minded—it was good to play the field and keep his options open. Life was too short to tie yourself down with one person, at least for him.

Gene was nodding toward the new girl. "How'd she do?" he asked Annette.

"She's terrific," Annette replied. "Fits right in, bantering with the customers, filling the orders and staying on top of things. She can actually count, which is handy. Remember that girl last year, Rhonda? She could not make change to save her life." Annette shook her head at the memory. "Seems comfortable in the setting too, which is a good thing. Where'd you find her?"

"She's a friend of Betsy Hanover, remember her?" As Annette nodded, Gene lifted his chin to include Donovan. "Betsy owns a BDSM club in Manhattan. Apparently Jaime was a regular there. I gave her an interview as a courtesy, and hired her out of desperation." He laughed. "I'm glad she's working out." He smiled wide at Annette. "You know I defer to you in that department."

"As you should, boy," Annette said, her dark eyes twinkling as she patted Gene's curly head. "And all other departments, too."

"Mistress," Gene sighed happily, nuzzling against her like a puppy.

Donovan reached for his bottle, draining it as he watched the girl approach the bar, carrying a tray filled with empty bottles, plates and crumpled napkins. He stood and lifted the hinged opening in the bar so she wouldn't have to walk around the side.

"Thanks," she said, moving past him and Annette, using her hip to open the swinging doors behind the bar that led into the kitchen.

"Frank's already gone for the night," Annette said as Jaime passed her with her tray. "Just put that stuff by the sink and he'll take care of it tomorrow. Want a beer before I shut down?"

Jaime reappeared, pushing her bangs from her forehead, though they immediately flopped back. "No, thanks. I'm so wiped out, if I had a beer I might have to spend the night here."

"How about a lemonade then? I have some left from a shandy I made earlier tonight."

Jaime hoisted herself onto the stool one down from Donovan. Without seeming to notice him, she leaned forward, placing her elbows on the bar. "Sure. That sounds great. Thanks."

Annette took a clean glass and scooped some crushed ice into it. She poured the lemonade over the ice and dropped in a maraschino cherry. While she was preparing the drink, Donovan turned to Jaime, extending his hand over the empty stool between them. "I'm Donovan Cartwright. Welcome aboard."

"Jaime Heller." Her grip was cool and firm, almost masculine in its assurance, which surprised Donovan. He realized he was expecting something softer and more demure and it threw him off balance.

Annette handed the drink to Jaime and Donovan noticed the girl's fingernails were short though nicely manicured and painted a pearly pink. As she lifted the glass, Donovan found himself watching her drink. Something about it was supremely erotic—the way her lips closed over the edge of the glass as she tilted her head back, her eyes closing, the long lashes brushing her cheeks, and the small, satisfied sigh after she'd drained the glass.

Donovan experienced a sudden nearly overwhelming urge to place his hand on her throat, thumb and forefinger tightening just beneath her jaw line, forcing her head back as he gripped a handful of her hair and lowered his mouth to hers. The image was so startlingly real that for a horrible moment he thought he'd actually done it. He must be more tired than he thought. He shook his head, shaking away the fantasy as if it were a physical presence in his brain.

Annette stepped out from behind the bar. She nodded toward Jaime and Donovan. "See you tomorrow." Turning to Gene, she added, "I'm going to change. See you in a minute?"

"Yes, Mistress," Gene said quietly, and Donovan noted the sudden lift of Jaime's eyebrows, though she gave no other outward sign she had heard him.

As Annette headed through the dungeon door, Gene stood and walked around Donovan to Jaime. "Annette's pleased with your work, Jaime. We'll see you tomorrow at eight?"

"You will." Jaime smiled, and Donovan noticed the deep dimple in her left cheek. Her skin looked satiny soft. His fingers, rough and calloused from years of working with his hands, itched to stroke her cheek.

Bending over, Jaime pulled off one of her high heels. "But these have got to go. I think I crippled myself tonight." She laughed, a full-throated laugh that made Donovan wonder if she was as vocal in bed.

"No problem," Gene agreed. "Flats are fine." He turned to Donovan. "Front door's locked and everyone's gone for the night. Will you set the alarm and see Jaime out to her car?"

"Of course," Donovan agreed, watching Gene leave. He looked at the clock behind the bar. It was 2:20 and normally at this hour he was done, but for some reason the fatigue he'd felt a moment before had lifted. A kind of nervous energy moved in his blood, as if he'd just had a double shot of espresso. It didn't take a rocket scientist to realize it was the sexy little sprite sitting one stool over that was the cause.

Though he had no particular plans to take it further, there was no harm in a little casual flirtation. He'd just push a few of her buttons—test the submissive waters, as it were.

He slid to the stool next to hers. "I saw you watching me tonight during the bondage wheel scene. You looked like a little girl in a candy store. Ever been on a wheel?"

"You saw me in that crowd?"

He grinned at her diversion tactic and ratcheted the flirtation up a notch. "I saw the longing in your face even from a distance. You were imagining the snug grip of those cuffs around your wrists, your thighs, your ankles and waist. Your body was aching to be stretched taut, at the mercy of my dominance. Your skin was tingling with the need to feel the stroke of my cane."

He paused to see if he was getting to her, looking for the flush on her cheeks, the dilation of her pupils, the parting of her lips in startled but aroused surprise.

Instead, to his chagrin, she tossed her head and snorted. "Ha! Are *you* ever off the mark. I eat boys like you for dinner and spit out the bones. I'm as dominant as you are. If I looked like a kid in a candy shop, it was only because *I* wanted to be the one with the cane in my hand, a boy toy strapped to the wheel as he begged me sweetly for another lick of fire. In fact, I bet you would fit up there quite nicely."

For a moment Donovan was speechless. Admittedly he'd laid it on a little thick in an effort to get a rise out of her. But when he'd seen Jaime in the crowd clutching her water glass to her chest as if in prayer, her eyes shining, her expression rapt, he'd pegged her for a sub, no question about it.

Now he just shrugged, only the lift of his eyebrows suggesting his disbelief. "My mistake," he said, standing and bowing slightly in her direction. "I'll wait for you by the changing room, *Mistress*."

"Glad we cleared that up," Jaime replied with another saucy flounce of her head.

But then he saw it, and he knew what he was seeing, no matter how much she protested to the contrary. She couldn't hide the telltale flush that was indeed rising along her chest and throat and pinkening her cheeks, even as her green eyes flashed with defiance.

Donovan followed her through the dungeon, stopping to spin the bondage wheel as they passed it. They locked eyes. Jaime was the first to turn away.

Donovan just smiled. He always did love a challenge.

# Chapter 3

Jaime stood in the middle of the garage apartment and did a slow three-sixty of the small space, spreading out her arms as if she could embrace the room. Who knew it could be so easy to uproot her life? Was finding a job and a place to stay right off the bat some kind of good omen? Jaime chose to think so.

Mary's cousin, Lucy, called two days after Jaime had arrived in San Francisco and gave Jaime directions to the place. Jaime showed up armed with plenty of cash. Lucy had rented the apartment to her on the spot, tucking the wad of bills into her bra with a broad grin and a handshake. "Mary says you're good people," Lucy had informed her. "That's good enough for me."

It was a single room over a garage with a small bathroom tucked into one corner and a galley kitchen along one side of the room that consisted of a mini refrigerator, a counter with a microwave, a small electric stove and a few cabinets bolted into the wall.

Though the place was less than half the size of her apartment in New Jersey, somehow it seemed bigger.

Maybe it was because of the large windows on the east and south walls that revealed the rolling hills and woods behind the structure, and gave play each morning to a gorgeous sunrise. Or maybe it was because the only furniture Jaime had acquired so far was a mattress and box spring, two old beanbag chairs and a small kitchen table and two chairs, all of which she'd bought secondhand at a thrift shop.

The apartment wasn't that far from the club, another good omen in Jaime's mind. She arrived at work a little early on Friday evening. After their initial flirtation her first night there, Jaime hadn't seen Donovan. He hadn't come to the club Wednesday or Thursday, apparently having some other obligation. Jaime tried not to speculate about where the professional Dom might be, or who he was with. After all, it was none of her business—she barely knew the guy.

The dungeon had been somewhat quiet as a result of his absence, with no sexy shows by the Master to draw the attention and admiration of the players and the gawkers alike.

Jaime changed into her uniform and knocked on Gene's open office door. He looked up from his laptop with a smile. "Hey, there. Come on in." Gene waved toward a chair. "What's up?"

After greeting him, Jaime said, "I was thinking." She spoke quickly to keep from losing her nerve. "When Donovan's out, I wouldn't mind stepping in.

You know—I could handle a public scene or two. Kick up the action a little on his days off."

Gene lifted his eyebrows and steepled his fingers beneath his chin. "Go on."

"I was thinking it might add a new dimension to have a Mistress onboard. Not that I need to tell you," she added, recalling his murmured *Yes, Mistress* to Annette her first night at the club, "but in my experience there are plenty of male subs eager to scene, and never enough Dommes out there ready to take them on."

Gene regarded her for a long moment. Jaime sat quietly, hoping she projected an air of confidence. Finally he said, "The club's reputation hangs on what the Master does. He's the reason we've made a name for ourselves as more than just another hangout for kinksters to get their rocks off."

Jaime nodded. She knew Gene was probably right, but being bathed in the atmosphere of the BDSM club these past couple of nights had left her aching to flex her whip arm and feel the warm press of a sub boy's lips on her foot as he thanked her for the session. If she got paid in the process, so much the better.

"Maybe I could do scenes on a smaller scale," she offered. "We could charge for my scenes and they could take place in one of the private play rooms. I could split the take with the house."

"And who would cover for you while you were off playing Pro Domme for fun and profit?"

Jaime took a breath, aware Gene would probably wonder where the hell she got off offering suggestions after having worked there less than a week. But what the hell, what did she have to lose? "We could hire another waitress? Part time? Don't you agree it would add a new dimension to the club, having a Mistress on the staff to complement the Master?"

Gene lifted his hands as if in defeat and laughed. "I have to admire your balls. Not even here a week and already you're gunning for a promotion."

"Oh, well I didn't mean to—"

"No, it's okay. It's cool. I actually kind of like the idea. But I have to run it by my partner. Donovan will be back tonight. We'll talk it over and let you know." He glanced at his watch and stood. "Doors open in an hour. Let's get to it."

~*~

Linda lay on her back in a sturdy black mesh hammock, her arms and legs raised high and spread wide, secured in Velcro cuffs dangling from thick rope knotted into bolts in the ceiling. With her spread legs facing the audience, her voluptuous form was positioned to leave nothing to the imagination—her dark gumdrop nipples perking in the center of her large breasts, her shaven pussy exposed between her ample thighs.

Linda, a highly responsive submissive, was one of Donovan's favorite scene partners, as she always gave the audience a good show. She was a wonderful pain slut and could orgasm at the drop of a hat, both from pleasure and erotic pain.

Six red Japanese hot wax drip candles designed especially for BDSM wax play stood in tall brass candlesticks on the side of the stage. A snake of eager volunteers was lined up and waiting, each eager for their chance to drop melted wax on the naked, bound woman. At Donovan's signal, a dozen or so men and women stepped up onto the stage one at a time. Selecting a candle, they held it over Linda's body under Donovan's watchful eye. Linda sighed with each droplet, as if it were a loving caress, rather than a burn on her skin.

When everyone who wanted to had taken a turn, Donovan lit a new candle, this one white, a nice contrast to her dark skin, which was the color of rich, creamy chocolate. He held the candle over Linda's breasts, letting the hot wax thoroughly coat her nipples before dripping a trail down her body as she twitched, gasped and sighed.

A few of the more daring volunteers had let some of the red wax drip onto her spread labia. Donovan held the white candle close above her cunt and let the melted liquid fall in hot splashes on the tender folds. Linda squealed and yelped as Donovan coated her cunt with white wax. He could feel the yearning in the crowd—some of them longing to feel the searing, sensual burn of the wax, others aching to inflict it.

Glancing out at the audience as he worked, Donovan saw Jaime standing in the back of the crowd, a fist to her mouth, her eyes wide as saucers. Did that look of longing in her eyes stem from a desire to do what he was doing, or to experience it?

He grinned inwardly at the memory of her hot denial when he'd suggested she might like to submit to his dominance. *Me thinks the lady doth protest too much* had come to mind, though he hadn't called her on it at the time.

He'd been looking forward to seeing her the next night and upping the ante of their flirtation. If he could have gotten out of his obligation to run the two-day seminar for a power exchange group in Los Angeles, he would have done it in a heartbeat. Well, he was back now, and damned if the girl wasn't glued to the stage, watching his every move with hungry eyes.

*Let's see what you think of this, Mistress Jaime.* Setting the candle carefully back in its holder, Donovan selected a single tail whip from the rack. "Slave Linda," he said in a voice loud enough for the spectators gathered around the stage to hear, "are you ready for me to remove the wax from your body?"

"Yes, Sir," Linda replied in a breathy rasp.

He held the whip so she could see it. "Shall I use this to whip it away, slave girl?"

"Oh, *yes*, please, Master. Please." Linda's dark eyes were shining, her body trembling in anticipation.

The room was silent as Donovan positioned himself beside the bound woman. He focused first on her breasts, alternating between the two mounds as he flicked at the hardened wax, causing it to crack and chip away with each stinging stroke.

When he could, Donovan stole glances at Jaime, who remained on the edge of the crowd, her body leaning toward the stage as if pulled by some kind of magnetic force. He still couldn't decide from her expression if she wanted to do what he was doing, or have it done to her.

Returning his focus to the luscious naked woman bound before him, Donovan flicked the tail down Linda's body, sending bits of red and white wax flying over the stage. Linda writhed and moaned, sweat glistening beneath her arms and on her forehead, her eyes squeezed closed. Donovan leaned close, murmuring for her ears only, "Are you okay, Linda? Do we continue? We can stop now if you've had enough. You did great." He stroked her cheek. Her skin was fever-hot.

Linda opened her eyes, fixing them on his face. "More," she begged in a throaty voice. "I want more."

Nodding, Donovan returned his focus to her cunt. He struck her between the legs with the tip of the whip, shattering the wax, which fell in pieces to the stage. Linda squealed, a long, peeling sound that echoed through the room. He continued to flick her with the whip, keeping the sting purposefully light on her tender flesh.

Linda's entire body began to shake, her toes curling, her fingers gripping tightly to the ropes above the cuffs. "Oh, god, oh yes, oh please, oh fuck, oh yesssssss!" she cried, her chest and neck flushing red as she orgasmed to the stroke of the single tail.

Finally she lolled her head to the side, her mouth agape, her hands limp, and Donovan dropped the whip. The room erupted into applause and raucous whoops of approval. Looking to the front of the crowd, Donovan nodded toward Linda's partner, Rose, who leapt up the three steps and raced to Linda's side, wrapping her arms around the naked woman.

"You did so good," Rose crooned, kissing Linda's face over and over between her words. "My sexy slave girl, you did so good."

Several men also joined them on the stage, helping to lower the hammock and release Linda from her bonds. Rose knelt beside her lover and spread a special salve over her skin, spending extra time on her labia, as Linda moaned and sighed her approval.

Donovan glanced out again to gauge Jaime's reaction, but she was gone.

~*~

If she'd thought she was busy the first three nights, they were nothing compared to Friday. Jaime barely had a chance to breathe from the minute the club opened. Her one consolation was that the busier she became, the more tips found their way into her apron.

She'd been startled with just how thrilled she was to learn Donovan would be back and doing a show that night. During her break, she'd slipped immediately into the dungeon to catch his first scene, trying to tell herself her interest was professional—she could learn a few things from the Master in case the partners agreed her idea to work as a pro Domme was a good one.

She'd embarrassed herself by gasping along with the woman on the stage as the melted wax dropped on her spread pussy. Thank goodness no one around her had noticed—everyone was riveted to the scene in front of them. Watching him wield the single tail with such precision and erotic skill had unnerved her, and she had fled, confused by her reactions and desires.

*It's just because he's so good at what he does,* she told herself as she handed an order across the bar to Annette. *It's not that you want him or want to experience for yourself what he does, it's that you want to be him.* But her hands were shaking as she set the drinks down in front of customers.

She found herself glad to be so busy. It left her little time to obsess about the man so effortlessly controlling the crowd in the dungeon beyond the bar.

Finally it was time for last call. Donovan and Gene were working in the dungeon, cleaning the equipment and storing toys while Annette did her bar work. Tommy helped Jaime bring the remaining dishes to the kitchen and wipe down the tables.

When they were done it was nearly three in the morning. Jaime was beat, but as she had each night so far, she experienced a kind of fierce satisfaction she'd never felt at the bank.

Frank, the cook, and Tommy were the first to leave, followed soon after by Gene and Annette. Jaime was disappointed Gene hadn't approached her about her idea, but she held her tongue. Probably he hadn't had time to talk it over yet with Donovan.

Jaime could have followed Annette when she changed, and walked out to the parking lot with Gene and Annette, but instead she lingered, nursing a glass of ice water at the bar, all too aware of Donovan, who was still moving around in the dungeon.

When the back door clicked shut, Donovan appeared in the doorway of the bar. "Oh," he said, acting surprised. "You still here?"

"Like you didn't know," Jaime retorted with a grin, lifting her chin. What was it about this guy that made her act like a teenager?

Coming into the room, Donovan lifted the hinged section of the bar and stepped behind it. Taking a glass, he scooped some ice and squirted cola into it. He raised the glass, tilting his head back as he drank. Jaime found herself staring at his Adam's apple as he swallowed. She tried to place a slave collar around his throat in her mind's eye, but the image refused to materialize.

Setting down the empty glass, Donovan hoisted himself up over the bar, dropping his legs beside Jaime and slipping down onto the stool beside her. Jaime stiffened, readying herself for him to give her a hard time over her reaction while watching the wax scene earlier that evening.

But to her surprise he said, "Gene mentioned the idea of you doing some private scenes with paying customers. We need to talk it over more, but I'm onboard with the idea in theory, provided you know what you're doing."

He was sitting close to her, his shoulder nearly touching hers. Along with the delicious scent of leather, she could smell his skin, an earthy combination of sweat and soap with a touch of something citrusy. She found herself leaning into the hard muscle of his shoulder and it was an act of sheer will to pull away.

Jaime reached for her water glass, holding it between them like a shield. "I've been playing the club scene in New York City for about five years," she said. "Like I told Gene, I know my way around a whip."

Donovan turned on the stool to face her. "What're you doing tomorrow afternoon, say around four?"

"Around four?" Jaime echoed stupidly. Was he asking her out?

"Yeah. I'm thinking we could meet here. I have a good friend who happens to be a serious pain slut and is always up for BDSM play. You could give me a demonstration of your skill set as a Domme—how you handle a whip, how you set up a scene, aftercare and the like. You can bring your own gear, or we have a full arsenal of toys available here for you to use. That work for you?"

"Yes. That works for me." Jaime's mind leaped forward, already planning various scenes in her head with which to impress the Master. She would use a ball stretcher, adding weights in increments to either side of the thick metal ring. She would have the pain slut bend over, legs spread, while she popped his ass and hanging balls with a single tail. With the ball stretcher still in place, she would truss his cock and balls with thin, strong rope and tie the rope to a hook in the wall or ceiling. She would warn him to stay very still as she flogged him, if he valued his family jewels.

"Excellent," Donovan replied, pulling Jaime out of her fantasy. "Give me your cell number. I just need to confirm with Rita. If she's available, we'll meet here tomorrow afternoon."

"Wait," Jaime blurted, confused. "What? Rita?"

Donovan lifted his eyebrows, his mouth curving in a sardonic smile. "Her name is Rita, yes. Is there a problem?"

"Yes, I mean, no. That is, I wasn't expecting a woman. The idea I discussed with Gene was for *male* subs." She started to say she'd only ever dommed men, and had zero interest in women, but stopped herself, not wanting to lose the opportunity to become more than a waitress at the club.

Donovan's smile had edged into a full out grin. "I'm not setting you up on a date, Jaime. This is an audition—a chance to show your skills as a Domme. What difference could it possibly make if the sub is male or female?" The grin faded. "Now," he said, crossing his arms over his chest. "You want to do this, or not?"

He was right. What difference did it make? This wasn't casual play at a club designed to get her off. She would be offering a professional service. Admittedly, CBT was out, but she could still show

Donovan she knew her way around rope and leather, and understood the psyche of a sub and knew how to give them what they wanted, and even better, what they needed.

She shook her head, smiling. "No, of course, you're right. It makes no difference. Yes, I want to do it." Reaching into her apron pocket, she pulled out the order pad and scrawled her cell phone number on it. Tearing off the sheet, she handed it to Donovan.

As he took it, their fingers brushed, his touch sending an unexpected jolt of something like electricity through her fingertips. She pulled her hand back, startled, and only just stopped herself from putting her fingers to her lips.

*Oh shit,* she thought with an inward groan. *I'm falling for a Dom.*

# Chapter 4

Jaime looked seriously hot in the black satin corset that accentuated her curves. Her black leather pants molded like a second skin to slender legs and a cute little ass. Velvet ribbons were laced in a vertical row of X's along the front of the corset, ending in a bow just between her breasts. Donovan's fingers actually itched with the desire to pluck the bow loose and let her breasts tumble free.

*Down boy.*

Donovan willed away the hard-on that was threatening. He was here to observe, nothing more. And so far, so good. Jaime had arrived a few minutes after Rita, and when Donovan introduced the two of them, Jaime pointed to her stiletto-clad feet and said in a haughty but at the same time sexy voice, "Greet me properly, slave girl." Rita had dropped at once to her knees and kissed the top of Jaime's pretty feet.

Before meeting that afternoon, Jaime and Donovan had a long telephone conversation regarding Rita's limits, likes and dislikes so Jaime could jump right in with the scene. Donovan had been impressed by Jaime's questions and observations, all of which showed she knew her way around a dungeon and had a good understanding of what made submissives tick. Of course he still planned to pay close attention during the actual session. If they did end up hiring Jaime to provide private scenes for club members, he wanted to be damn sure she knew what she was doing.

Jaime spoke to the woman kneeling at her feet. "Tell me your safeword, Rita."

"Red light, Mistress."

"Very good," Jaime replied, her eyes briefly meeting Donovan's before returning to look down at the woman kneeling before her. "The Master has told me of your limits, your passions and your fears. I am going to push your sensual envelope, Rita. I want to take you to the very edge of what you think you can handle, and if you prove yourself worthy, I'll help you move past it." There was power in Jaime's voice and a confidence Donovan hadn't heard before.

"Yes, Mistress. Thank you, Mistress," Rita replied.

*Sensual envelope,* Donovan thought. *I like that.*

Jaime touched Rita's shoulder. "You may rise," she said imperiously.

When Rita stood, Donovan saw that the nipples on her ample breasts, bare beneath the sheer white robe she wore, had hardened into points and her features had softened into a submissive gaze he knew well.

The three of them moved to one of the private play areas. Along with a rack of whips and floggers, the room was equipped with a St. Andrew's cross and a padded spanking bench. Donovan hadn't told Jaime what room they would use, wanting to see how well she improvised.

Without missing a beat, Jaime pointed to the bench. "Drop the robe and lie facedown," she said to Rita.

Without hesitation Rita untied the sash and let her robe fall to the ground. She draped her body gracefully over the center bar of the spanking bench, positioning her knees and forearms on the padded rests that paralleled either side of the center bar.

Donovan moved to one wall, standing where he would have a good view of the scene. Pressing the sole of one of his boots against the wall for balance, he leaned against it, crossing his arms over his chest. He had given up trying to fight the erection bulging in his jeans. He'd have to be dead not to react to the erotic scene before him—Jaime in her sexy Dominatrix outfit and Rita, her shapely ass creamy white against the black leather of the bench, waiting to be whipped to a rosy red.

Jaime moved toward the toy bag she'd brought with her, but Donovan shook his head. "Pick something from the rack. Sometimes clients bring their own toys. I'd like to see how you handle something you might be less familiar with."

A flicker of annoyance moved over Jaime's face, but it was gone as quickly as it had arrived. With a cool smile, she nodded and moved toward the whip rack. She selected a medium flogger and returned to Rita. She dragged the leather tresses over Rita's bare back and ass. "The Master has told me you love the sting of leather and the cut of the cane."

With her other hand, Jaime stroked Rita's cheek. Donovan sucked in a surprised breath when Jaime suddenly slapped the cheek she'd been caressing a moment before.

Rita gasped and then sighed. "Ooooh," she breathed, "thank you, Mistress."

Jaime slapped her again, leaving the imprint of her small hand on Rita's cheek. "You're welcome."

When they'd talked on the phone, Donovan hadn't mentioned that Rita loved having her face slapped, but somehow Jaime had intuited it. Though Rita probably had a good ten to fifteen years on Jaime, there was no question Jaime was completely in charge of the scene so far and, in spite of himself, Donovan was impressed.

Still holding the flogger, Jaime flicked her wrist, letting the tresses land with a slap on Rita's ass. Rita moaned and wriggled her bottom, clearly wanting more. Jaime obliged, striking Rita hard over both cheeks before moving to the backs of her thighs. As Jaime whipped the woman, she continued to speak, her voice low and seductive.

"The Master told me you need the erotic pain to fully experience the pleasure. You need to suffer, don't you, Rita? It's what you were born for. It's who you are."

"Yes, Mistress. Please, Mistress."

Jaime flogged her harder and Rita moaned. Donovan wanted take the flogger from Jaime's hands. But not to whip the naked, eager sub girl kneeling over the spanking bench. No, he wanted to place Jaime there instead. He wanted to rip away her sexy bustier and slide those soft leather pants down her legs. He ached to explore the longing he'd seen in her face when she'd watched his shows. He wanted to uncover the secret submissive he was almost sure she kept hidden behind that masterful façade. Was it hidden so deeply even she didn't know it was there?

*Stay in the moment,* he reminded himself. *This isn't about you.*

After several minutes of flogging, Rita began to gyrate against the bench, grinding her bare cunt against the leather. Donovan would have stopped her from such overt self-stimulation without express permission, but Jaime did not.

Instead she replaced the whip in the rack and selected a cane. Without warning, Jaime struck Rita's ass hard, the sound of the cane against skin cracking like a gun's report. Rita jerked and squealed, her gyrations momentarily interrupted.

"Don't stop, slut," Jaime ordered, painting another dark red line across Rita's already rosy ass with the cane. "You take your pleasure without asking. I'll give you pain in the same way."

Donovan was surprised by her action—it was their first session, after all, and he would have expected Jaime to start slowly with what was a potentially dangerous implement. Rita's flesh was already welting where the cane had landed, the welts rapidly darkening from red to purple. He leaned forward, ready to intervene if Jaime went too far, but Rita seemed to be handling it well. Rita continued to masturbate herself against the leather, her hips swiveling provocatively as Jaime added three more welts to the ample target of her ass.

"Take it, slut," Jaime ordered, her voice now a little breathless as she danced around the sub girl, expertly wielding the cane. "Suffer for me." Donovan could smell the rising scent of Rita's lust perfuming the small room. He caught a glimpse of her glistening cunt as she gyrated against the spanking bench, squealing with each cut of Mistress Jaime's exacting cane.

Donovan found himself trying to catch Jaime's eye, but she was totally absorbed in her task, which of course was as it should be. As the Mistress caned the sub girl, Rita moaned and trembled against the spanking bench, her toes curling and uncurling with each stroke. Donovan pressed his palm against his crotch in an effort to ease the pressure building there.

"Do it, slut," Mistress Jaime said suddenly. "Come for me. Now!"

The cane whipped through the air, landing in a blur of slicing strokes. Rita began to wail, a high-pitched keening sound that blended pleasure and pain as her body shuddered in convulsive climaxes. Jaime didn't stop the caning until Rita lay limp against the bench, her body bathed in sweat.

Finally Jaime put down the cane. Crouching beside Rita, Jaime smoothed back her dark hair, which had fallen in a curtain over her face. Jaime stroked Rita's cheek and her back, and glided her fingers over the welts she'd raised on Rita's ass. "Are you okay? Did you have fun?"

Rita opened her eyes, which seemed to Donovan to be sparkling with submissive fire. Her face creased in a broad smile. "I'm more than okay, Mistress! That was *amazing*. It's like you were inside my soul, taking me just past the edge of what I could handle, but holding my hand in the process so I wasn't even scared. Does that make sense?"

Jaime nodded, drawing in and letting out a deep breath. "Yes. You pleased me, Rita. You're very responsive. I like that. You may kneel now and thank me properly."

Rita lifted herself from the bench and executed a kind of slow roll to the floor. Again she kissed the tops of Jaime's feet. This time when Jaime met Donovan's eye she offered a triumphant smile, and he smiled back, lifting a thumb of approval.

When Jaime touched Rita's head, Rita sat back on her haunches. She wrapped her arms beneath her large breasts as she twisted toward Donovan with a wide grin.

"She's fantastic, Sir. Can we do it again?"

Donovan laughed. "That's up to Mistress Jaime."

Turning to Jaime, he smiled and reached out to shake her hand, resisting the sudden impulse to pull her instead into his arms. "Congratulations. You've passed stage one of the audition."

~*~

"Okay, I'll bite," Jaime finally said, once Rita had dressed and left the club. "What did you mean, stage one?" They had moved from the dungeon and were seated side by side at the bar. While still riding high from the success of the scene, Jaime was uneasy as to just what stage two might be.

Donovan regarded her with his very blue eyes. They were the blue of a clear spring sky and somehow just as vast, contained only by the darker blue ring around each iris. And those eyelashes! Why was it always the men who got the great eyelashes?

She forced her gaze away from his face, lingering on the three snakes curling together around his arm beneath the short sleeve of his black T-shirt. The tattoo wasn't large, each of the three snakes no thicker than a pencil, bringing to Jaime's mind a DNA double helix, though with the addition of fangs and serpent tongues. Inked in black, turquoise and red, the snakes were skillfully rendered, and looked as if they might leap from his arm if she came too close.

"Stage one," Donovan replied, drawing her eyes back to his face, "was my assessment of your ability as a pro. You satisfied me that you have what it takes to execute a scene. But that's not all there is to being a Master, or in your case, a Mistress."

"I'm sorry. I'm not following."

"I'll explain more clearly in a second. First, though, I have to say, I was a little surprised at your decision to use the cane so soon into the scene, and with such force."

"It worked, didn't it?" Jaime retorted. "She loved it."

Donovan nodded. "She did, but it could have backfired. You don't know Rita personally. And you'll know even less about the clients who come to you at the club, especially at first. You're not going to have the luxury of a pre-scene briefing about a sub's likes and dislikes the way you had regarding Rita. You have to be careful not to go too far, too fast, especially in the kind of public, paid-for-hire scene we're talking about for the club."

Jaime ducked her head, embarrassed. "Got it," she said.

Donovan nodded. "What's your personal take on the cane versus the flogger or a single tail? Which do you prefer?"

Jaime thought about it, glad he'd changed the subject. "I like them all. It depends on what the sub wants, I guess, or what they need. I have less experience with a single tail than with the flogger or the cane, but I've done it a few times."

Donovan shook his head. "No, that's not what I mean. I mean which do you prefer to experience? To feel on your skin? What do you find erotic about one versus the other? What do you find frightening, or enticing?"

Jaime snorted. "Oh, I get what you're asking now. You're of the school of thought that you can't possibly understand the masochistic experience unless you subject yourself to the same treatment." She shook her head. "Sorry, I don't buy it. Not to be crass, but just because I don't have a cock, that doesn't mean I don't know my way around CBT, for example."

Donovan lifted the corners of his mouth in a small smile, but his eyes remained serious. "Point taken. But that's a very specific experience. Here's where stage two comes in. In my professional opinion, it's important to know everything you *can* know about how what you're doing impacts your sub. You have a special responsibility that goes above and beyond a typical relationship because of the vulnerability of the submissive during a scene." He spread his hands on the bar. They were large, powerful hands, the fingertips square, the nails short. "If you're going to flog someone, to whip them, to cane them, to drip hot wax on their skin, to clamp their nipples or bind them with rope, you should first experience it yourself."

"What, are you telling me *you've* experienced all those things?" Jaime tried to muster the image of the Master, naked and bound, his face twisted in erotic agony as the cane cut his skin, but she couldn't seem to manage it.

To her surprise, he nodded soberly. "Absolutely. My mentor insisted on it, and he was right. It deepens not only your intellectual knowledge, but your ability to empathize and connect with your sub. Whenever I trained dominants, it's a requirement."

Jaime wrapped her arms around her torso, shaking her head. "Not happening."

Donovan lifted his hands, palms upward, and shrugged. "That's entirely up to you, Jaime. If you want the job, though, it's not open for debate. There is no way I would hire someone who hasn't experienced on a personal level everything he or she does to another person in the context of BDSM play. Stage two involves you submitting to me in a controlled scene. It's important you experience firsthand what that feels like, both physically and mentally."

What the hell? Was he for real? He was bluffing — he had to be. Yeah, she believed he was sincere in what he was saying, but his experience wasn't necessarily the universal experience. He just needed to understand that. Yet, even while Jaime's head rejected the idea out of hand, her body was tingling with the possibilities. A sudden image of herself, naked and restrained on the bondage wheel, her heart pounding, nipples throbbing, cunt wet as she watched the Master lift the whip and then let the leather strike her bare skin, leaped into her mind's eye.

What was going on here? She took a deep breath and blew it out.

"I get what you're saying," she finally managed, pushing the image out of her consciousness as best she could. "But I just can't agree that this stage two thing is really necessary. You saw for yourself that I can handle a scene. You saw Rita's reaction. You heard her words — she can't wait to scene with me again." When Donovan didn't reply, Jaime continued, "Look, I think it's quite clear I can handle the job. I can give you references if you want. Betsy Hanover back in New York and any number of guys at her club for starters."

Donovan shook his head. "Sorry. We're talking deal breaker here." He slid from the stool and stood. "Not to worry, though. Annette's very satisfied with your work as a waitress. We'll just leave it at that. I'll set the alarm on my way out. There's a two minute exit delay, so don't linger too long."

Jaime watched, stunned, as Donovan walked out of the bar, heading through the dungeon toward the back door of the club. As he left, it was almost as if he took the oxygen in the room with him, leaving Jaime gasping for air.

Fuck! The dude was serious. She was going to blow it—she wasn't going to get the job. She'd be stuck serving beer and wiping down tables, when she could give more, so much more, to the club.

*Come on, Jaime. You can do it. What's the big deal? It's just the one time. Surely you can handle this one session with a trained Master. And maybe he's right. Maybe you can learn a thing or two. If it's going to make you a better Domme, why are you fighting it so hard? It's just a kind of rite of passage, a requirement to get the job. No big deal. Don't blow this, Jaime. Not when you're so close.*

Jaime leaped from the stool and ran through the dungeon. She could hear the sound of the alarm being set, a series of beeps as he entered the code. "Donovan! Wait. Come back. Let's talk a little more about this."

She came up behind him. Without turning to face her, Donovan said, "What's left to say?" But he punched in the code again, deactivating the alarm.

"Okay, okay," Jaime said. "I'll do it. I'll do a scene with you and experience the whip and whatever all you think is necessary. Okay? Do we have a deal?"

Donovan turned toward her, his eyes boring holes into her face. He lifted his hand and touched her cheek with two fingers. Jaime stepped back as if struck, drawing in a quick, involuntary breath at the power of his touch.

"Why are you fighting so hard, hmm? What's really going on beneath the surface, Jaime?" Donovan spoke gently, but held her captive with his gaze.

Flustered, Jaime finally managed to look away. "I don't know what you're talking about."

"I think you do. Come on, you don't have to pretend with me. I certainly won't think less of you as a Domme, if that's what you're worried about. There are plenty of dominants who are submissive in the right circumstance."

She turned back to glare at him. "Yeah, well, I'm not one of them."

Donovan shrugged. "Hey, if all this resistance is because you're afraid you might just discover I'm right about your submissive tendencies, don't worry. I won't hold it against you, I promise."

"Submissive tendencies!" Jaime blurted. "Are you nuts? I'm as dominant as you are. How many times do I have to tell you that?"

Donovan smiled, a maddeningly smug expression on his face. Jaime barely resisted the impulse to slap it away. "I've watched you all week, Jaime. Your reactions during my shows have given you away, even if you're not yet self-aware enough to recognize it."

He placed his hand on her arm and this time Jaime didn't pull away, even though she wanted to. She found herself rooted to the spot, Donovan's sexy, deep voice weaving a spell around her senses. "Listen to me, Jaime. I know you believe you're one-hundred percent dominant. Let's say for the sake of argument right now that you've never felt the desire to sexually submit to another person, that you've never ached to experience that kind of surrender."

"Never," Jaime asserted, though it came out as a whisper. His fingers wrapped around her arm sent sparkles of heat through her body, which hummed with a curious kind of energy.

"Fair enough. It's possible my instincts regarding you are off the mark, but I don't think so. So here's the deal. In order to get the job, you will scene with me, and I will help you experience the various modes of erotic torture you would use in your role as a Domme. If nothing else, the experience will make you a better dominant than you already are."

Finally he let go of her, stepping back. "But I bet you you're going to find it's more than just a pure act of will on your part to endure the scene to get the job. I bet it's going to take you to a place you never dreamed you would go."

"Yeah, well, you bet wrong," Jaime snapped, her strength and will returning now that he'd let her go.

Donovan regarded her with an amused air. "Okay then. Why don't we formalize it? Formalize the bet."

"Excuse me?"

"I bet you're going to get in touch with the submissive part of your psyche that's buried beneath the tough, sexy persona you project as a Domme. If at the end of the session, you can honestly tell me there's nothing there—that my instincts are wrong about the secret, aching need you have to submit, then you win the bet. But if"—he paused, waiting until she looked at him before continuing—"if it turns out there's even a germ of truth to my theory that you're submissive on some level, then I win."

All of a sudden Jaime's heart was beating way too fast and her mouth had gone dry. She could feel the tension in every muscle of her body, her fight or flight instincts on high alert. At the same time, she had an almost uncontrollable desire to throw herself into Donovan's arms and bury her face in his chest. Instead she just continued to stare stupidly at him.

"So?" he said softly. "You in?"

"What are the stakes," she finally managed to reply. "How do we decide who wins?"

"I'll take you through a scene. If I'm wrong and the experience leaves you cold, then you win. If it affects you, and believe me, we'll both know it if it does, then I win."

"And the prize?" Jaime asked faintly.

A curious gleam came into Donovan's eyes, making them look like blue flames. Jaime could feel his raw power, and her own impulse to yield to it. "Forty-eight hours," Donovan said. "Forty-eight hours serving as the other person's personal sex slave. If I win, you'll come stay with me for that time period, and submit one-hundred percent to whatever I choose, sexually and otherwise. If you win, I'll come to you and serve you in whatever way suits *you*, sexually or otherwise." He grinned. "If the sex part doesn't interest you, I'll be perfectly content to clean your house, wash your car, give you massages and foot rubs or paint your toenails. Whatever you want, I'll be your obedient slave boy."

The image of strong, sexy Donovan kneeling in a frilly white apron and nothing else, painting Jaime's toenails while she idly flicked him with a whip made Jaime grin. The thought of him naked and in her bed made her press her thighs together and bite her lower lip to keep from moaning. As long as the sex was on her terms, bring it on!

Jaime felt herself rallying and she shook off the strange languor that had suffused her senses a moment before. Of course she would win such a bet. No question about it.

"You're on," she said with a grin. "It's a bet. When should we schedule the scene? The club's closed tomorrow—"

"We're here now," Donovan interrupted. "Let's finish the audition, shall we?" Without giving her time to answer, he continued, "I need to run out for just a minute. I've seen you eyeing the bondage wheel all week. When I return, I expect to find you naked and waiting, arms and legs extended along the X." He leaned down, kissing her lightly on the cheek while she struggled to form a cohesive thought, much less give it utterance.

It wasn't until she heard the click of the back door as it automatically locked behind him that she finally managed to say, "What the hell?" Yet, even as she spoke, her legs moved her into the dungeon, and she realized she was heading for the wheel.

# Chapter 5

Donovan would have placed even money on what he might find when he reentered the club. He hadn't really had anywhere to go, but he wanted to give Jaime a chance to get her bearings and make her decision. As he entered the dungeon, he let his eyes move slowly toward the bondage wheel, his heart doing a sudden flip in his chest as he took in the sight of the naked girl facing forward, her arms and legs extended along the X exactly as he'd commanded.

Without speaking, he walked slowly through the room toward her, the click of his boots echoing against the hardwood floor. Jaime followed his approach with those wide, sage-green eyes, her cheeks and neck suffused with color, her chest rising and falling as she breathed from softly parted lips.

He could feel her tension like a palpable thing in the air between them, but also saw the resolve in her eyes and in the set of her jaw. As he came to a stop directly in front of her, he couldn't help but drink in her fragile, feminine beauty.

She had a narrow waist that only flared slightly at her girlish hips before curving again into the long, lean lines of her legs. Her breasts were heavy on her slender frame, lifted by her upraised arms and tipped with dark pink nipples that were standing at attention. A small, groomed triangle of red pubic hair, darker than the red-gold hair on her head, barely concealed the sweet cleft of her sex between her spread legs.

Donovan stroked her cheek, letting his fingers slide down her throat, feeling the shudder that passed through her body at his touch. He pressed his palm lightly against her chest. He could feel her heart pounding.

"Shh," he said, moving his hand again to her face. "There's no need to be afraid, Jaime. I won't give you more than you can handle. You've done this yourself a hundred times. You know that what I offer isn't about pain, per se, but about surrender. Surely you can take what you dish out, no?"

Mutely, she nodded, though he could tell she wasn't entirely convinced. Normally he would have insisted she answer properly and address him either as Master or Sir, but for now he let it go. After all, she hadn't agreed to submit to him, but only to experience firsthand the sensations she'd been so ready and willing to provide for others, without a real understanding of what it felt like to be on the receiving end.

Donovan wouldn't deny Jaime knew her way around a BDSM scene. She'd done an excellent job with Rita. She clearly had the gift of dominance, as well as the fire and skill needed to conduct a good scene. But he couldn't forget the haunted, hungry look in her eyes when she'd watched his shows, or the visceral reaction when he'd challenged her to take this chance. Yes, there was fear there, but there was also desire—he was sure of it.

"We'll start slowly," Donovan said, a surge of adrenaline ripping through his body at the thought of flogging this gorgeous naked young woman. "A nice warm-up flogging, okay?"

Again she only nodded, and again he let it pass.

"Turn around," he commanded. "Face the wheel, arms and legs against the X like before." He waited while she obeyed, his eyes lingering over the sight of her small, rounded ass. His cock hardened as he contemplated the various ways he would turn her skin from milky white to cherry red before the session was over.

"I'm just going to cuff your wrists for now," he informed her. "It's your job to maintain your position, feet flat." He chose the lower wrist cuffs so Jaime's feet could remain on the floor. He wrapped and clipped the leather cuffs around Jaime's wrists one at a time, a thrum of anticipation making his heart pop into a higher gear.

"Relax your hands," he admonished, noting her curling fingers. "You know better."

Stepping over to the rack, Donovan selected a heavy suede flogger. Jaime turned her head to the side. She was watching him, anxiety radiating from her like a force field. She was still breathing too fast and he moved closer, gently pressing his chest against her bare back as he spoke softly into her ear.

"Jaime, you need to slow your breathing. You can do this. I know you can. But if you're unsure that you want to continue, if you want to stop now, just say so. Your job as waitress is still waiting, and there'll be no hard feelings, I promise."

"No." Jaime's voice came out hoarse and she cleared her throat, repeating, "No. I want to do this. I want the job. If this is what it takes…" She let the sentence trail off.

*Yes,* he thought to himself. *This is what it takes, but there's more going on here. I'm sure of it.* Aloud, he said, "Okay, then. Deep breaths. Close your eyes and let go of your resistance. Show me the same grace you demand of your subs."

Jaime drew in a deep, shuddery breath. "That's it," he urged. "In…and out. In…and out. Better." Stepping back, he pressed his hands lightly against her shoulders. "Lower your shoulders. Stop holding all that tension. That's better. Just relax. Open yourself to the experience."

He began slowly, brushing her skin with the soft suede. He took his time, very slowly building the intensity until he gauged she was sufficiently calm.

Then, with a flick of his wrist, he let the first real stroke swish and sting against her ass.

Jaime yelped, her body tensing. Donovan struck her again, thrilling as he always did to the sound of leather against flesh, enjoying the jiggle of her ass with each stroke, and the rising color on her skin.

"Hey! It hurts!" Jaime cried, doing a little avoidance dance with her feet as she tried in vain to escape the stinging kiss of the flogger.

"It's supposed to, silly girl," Donovan chided with a grin. "Stay in position. Feet flat on the ground. Don't focus on the pain. Focus on where that pain can take you. Focus on the pleasure of pure sensation." He moved the flogger, letting the suede tresses wrap around her thighs and land between her shoulder blades before returning to her delectable ass.

Her yelps continued, but a sort of breathy quality began to infuse the sound, which segued from outraged cries of pain to something much more like the sweet moaning of a woman in the throes of orgasm.

*I knew it,* he thought triumphantly, though he recognized it was too soon to really make such a call.

Replacing the flogger in the rack, he returned to the girl and released her wrist cuffs. "Turn around and place your back to the wheel," he said. When Jaime didn't immediately react, he put a hand on her shoulder and spun her around. She brought her arms protectively over her breasts as she fell back against the padded leather. Donovan watched the play of emotions moving over her face, their meaning clear to him—part fear, part protest and, she couldn't hide it from him, part desire.

"Arms extended over your head along the X. I'm going to cuff you fully into the wheel. Since you have a hard time staying in position on your own, we'll just take away that option for now."

This time he secured her wrists in the higher cuffs, forcing her onto her toes. He buckled the waist belt in place and then secured her thighs and ankles along the X to hold her fast against the wheel, with the net result that her feet no longer touched the ground.

"How you doing, Jaime? Still okay?" Donovan asked as he stepped back to admire the view.

"I'm nervous," Jaime answered. "I feel very vulnerable."

Donovan nodded. "Yes, you are completely restrained, completely at my mercy. Takes a lot of trust, doesn't it? It's a lot to ask of someone, would you agree?"

Jaime nodded. "Yeah. I get it. The whole sub experience thing, how it's important to put myself in their shoes, or, uh, their cuffs." She flashed a sudden grin, though her eyes remained anxious. "I think you can let me down now."

Donovan smiled, shaking his head. "You think wrong. We're just getting started."

Reaching into his back pocket, he pulled out a pair of clover clamps. "You know what these are, right?"

"Yes," Jaime whispered, her eyes widening as she stared at them. "Is this really necessary?"

"It really is."

Donovan reached for one of her perfect nipples, his mouth watering as he fantasized about closing his lips over the soft marble of flesh and making it harden with his tongue. Instead he rolled it in between finger and thumb, pulling it taut. He glanced at her face. Her lips were pressed into a single line, her brows furrowed, nostrils flaring.

"Jaime, look at me." She shifted her gaze, her eyes interlocking with his. "You need to calm down. You took the flogging well. It's not necessary to white-knuckle through the experience the way you appear to be doing. Follow the advice you give your subs. Embrace the experience. Savor the eroticism to be found in what I'm giving you. *Let go.*"

Jaime nodded slowly, her mouth relaxing a little, some of the panic easing from her expression.

Donovan stroked her satiny soft cheek, the lyrics from that Radiohead song, *Creep*, moving through his head: *you're just like an angel, your skin makes me cry.*

He lost his concentration, and had to remind himself this was about Jaime, not himself.

He reached again for her nipple, which had hardened to a stiff point, perfect for the clamp. Pressing the clamp open, Donovan positioned it carefully on either side of the dark pink nubbin, getting as close to the base as he could before letting it close.

Predictably, Jaime yelped. Ignoring this, Donovan did the same to her other nipple and then stepped back once more to admire his handiwork. She looked incredibly sexy with the clamps compressing each reddening nipple, the silver chain swaying between her lovely, full breasts. There were tears in her eyes, her cheeks and chest mottled with color, her breath again rasping in her throat.

Donovan knew from personal experience how much the clover clamps could hurt. "Hey," he said gently. "You're doing really, really good. You know, right, that the pain gets easier to bear as your nerve endings numb?"

"It hurts," Jaime whispered, pleading with her eyes.

If she were his lover, he would have crouched now between her legs, spreading her sex with his hands and pulling her hips forward so he could taste the spicy sweetness of her cunt. That would distract her from the pain, he was sure of it.

Of course, that wasn't an option. Instead, he began to spin the wheel, very slowly. Jaime gasped, her body visibly tensing. "Relax," Donovan urged. "You're completely secure in the cuffs." He continued to turn the wheel until she was upside down. The chain between the nipple clamps fell downward, glinting silver against her throat.

"It's not so bad now, right? Your nipples are numbing about now." To further distract her, and because he wanted to, Donovan stroked the soft skin of her inner thighs. Jaime shuddered at his touch, and he could feel her desire radiating from her skin like heat—or was it his own desire he felt? How easy it would be to let his fingers continue their slow glide to the sweet pooch of her sex so enticingly displayed between her spread legs. Was she wet, in spite of her fear? Because of it?

He turned the wheel until she was once again upright. "I'm going to take them off now, okay?"

Jaime bit her lower lip and furrowed her brows. She knew, of course, what was in store for her. Slowly she nodded.

Donovan reached for both clamps, releasing them at the same time.

"Fuck!" Jaime screamed as the blood flow returned to her tortured nipples.

Donovan hid his smile as he cupped her breasts, moving his palms gently over the engorged, tender nipples, soothing away the pain. "Pretty intense, huh?" he offered, stating the obvious. Jaime didn't reply.

When he gauged she was sufficiently recovered, Donovan unbuckled the belt and released the cuffs, helping Jaime regain her footing as she stepped away from the wheel.

"You're doing really well so far," he said.

"So far?" Jaime blurted. "You mean we aren't done yet? Come on, Donovan. I can't take much more of this."

"Sure you can, Jaime. Don't sell yourself short." Donovan grinned.

"But—"

He put two fingers to her lips, shaking his head. "No buts, Jaime. We're not done yet. Turn to face the wheel, arms and legs against the X." Again she opened her mouth to protest but he spoke first. "Just think about Rita. She's probably got the club on speed dial by now, just itching to get the first pro session with Mistress Jaime. And once the word is out, you're going to be as busy as I am, you can count on it. You don't want to just be a Domme who goes through the motions, without the deeper level of real understanding you can attain if you choose to, do you? Don't quit before the miracle, Jaime. Give the process a chance."

Jaime closed her mouth, the glint of determination again appearing in her eyes, her small, square chin jutting forward in a show of defiant courage.

"That's the spirit," he said. "There is nothing sexier to me than a strong submissive."

"I'm not—" Jaime began.

"I know, I know. You're not a sub. So you say." Donovan pointed to the wheel. "Go on, get in position facing the wheel."

To her credit, Jaime obeyed without further protest, staying quiet and still as Donovan again locked her into the cuffs. Securing her at the ankle and wrists, he used the lower cuffs this time, allowing her to remain standing, her toes snugged in the space between the wheel and the floor.

Returning to the rack, he selected one of the thicker canes, which he knew would be easier for a novice to handle than one of the thinner, whippier canes that marked the skin far more easily. "I'm going to introduce you to the cane, Jaime. As you know intellectually, it's very different from the diffused sensation of a many-tressed flogger. The impact of a cane, because of its shape and material, is very focused, very intense."

He started slowly to warm and ready her skin, just tapping the fleshiest part of her ass for several minutes until he felt her relax, her muscles easing, her breathing slowed to something approaching normal. He began then to hit her a little harder, just enough to get her attention. He tapped the cane in steady, even strokes over the small, fleshy globes of her cute little ass.

Just a slight increase in intensity caused her to squirm and gasp, though she couldn't move much, bound along the X as she was. He struck her harder, causing a long pink line to rise on her left cheek. For symmetry's sake, he added a second line on the right cheek.

"Jesus!" Jaime cried. "This fucking *hurts*, Donovan. I can't do it. It's too much."

"It's not enough," Donovan countered. "You aren't letting go." He relented though, and set down the cane. He placed his hands gently on Jaime's ass. As he stroked her hot skin he murmured, "Think about what you said to Rita. Remember? Something about pushing her sensual envelope. I liked what you said, Jaime. And that's what it's really about, isn't it? Sensuality. Touch. Connection."

He continued to stroke her skin, letting his fingers trail along the backs of her thighs. However much she protested that she wanted him to stop, he could feel her desire, sense her need. He could smell the spicy, delicate scent of her musk, and feel the throb of his own cock.

Jesus god, he wanted this woman. As much to distract himself from the nearly uncontrollable urge to touch the wetness he was sure he'd find between her legs, he again picked up the cane.

He warmed her skin, moving more quickly this time to a level of intensity he knew was hard for her to take, certain, though, that it wasn't too much. He felt in perfect control now, master of his game, ready to take her where she needed to go.

He stepped to the side, drawing his arm back and letting the cane crack against her skin, this time leaving not just a line, but a rising welt.

Jaime screamed.

Power surged through Donovan's body, pooling in his throbbing cock. At the same time, a deep, fierce tenderness filled him, and he wanted in the worst way to take this trembling, sexy woman into his arms. He wanted to kiss away the pain he himself had inflicted only a moment before. He was surprised by the intensity of his own reaction with a woman he barely knew. He needed to rein in his feelings.

*Focus on the scene.*

"What was it you said to Rita, Jaime? You wanted to take her to the edge of what she thought she could handle, right? And if she proved herself worthy" —he struck her again, adding a second welt—"you would help her move past it, to a place of true submission, true surrender." Jaime's hands were clenched into fists over the cuffs. "Let me do that for you," Donovan urged. "Let me take you where you've always needed to go."

He set down the cane and reached for a long-handled riding crop. He smacked the looped rectangle of leather against Jaime's ass, a steady thwacking against one cheek and then the other, the sound punctuated by her breathy, mewling cries.

Her ass was a lovely cherry red now, with several beautiful welts on each cheek. Her breathing had deepened and slowed, the panic easing from her body as she began to surrender at last.

He reached once more for the flogger, and began to flog her body from ass to shoulder and back again in a steady rain of stinging leather. She groaned, a guttural, primal sound, utterly feminine and deeply arousing. It was all Donovan could do to stay focused, but he managed through an act of sheer will.

He continued to flog her, even harder than before. Jaime moaned softly with each stroke. Her head had fallen back. Her lips were parted, her eyes closed. Her fingers were unfurled, her body limp, though held fast in its bonds.

"Yes," Donovan whispered in awe, thrilled as he always was by a submissive's total surrender. He continued for a few minutes longer, slowly easing the stroke of leather until it was back to a gentle caressing swish, soft as butter against her heated skin.

Finally he set the flogger down and released Jaime from her bonds. "You did it, Jaime. I knew you could."

~*~

Jaime drifted in an altered state—not quite conscious and yet at the same time keenly aware of what was going on around her. She felt a deep sense of utter wellbeing. The feeling was unfamiliar and yet welcome, as if she'd been seeking it without knowing it, unaware of its lack until this moment. She let herself fall back into Donovan's arms, as trusting as a baby that he would catch her.

He carried her across the dungeon into one of the private aftercare rooms. He settled on the sofa and gently deposited Jaime beside him. She would rather have stayed in his arms, curling into him like a child as he held her close.

No longer in the safe confines of Donovan's strong embrace, some of the sensual lethargy that had settled over Jaime's senses like a soft, snug blanket began to burn away and she suddenly remembered she was naked. There was a folded sheet on the cushion beside her, and Jaime reached for it, wrapping it around herself.

The skin on her back and especially her ass was still burning from the extended session. The experience had been at once scary and powerful. She had to admit she had a new level of respect for the subs who knelt so willingly at her feet. By the same token, she was deeply shaken by her own reaction to the scene, though she couldn't yet tease out what part of it was simple sexual attraction to the sexy man seated beside her, and what part meant more.

"So," Donovan said, pulling her from her reverie. "You get it now, huh? You see there's more to this whole D/s thing than maybe you thought?"

Jaime turned to face him. "I have to admit, Donovan, I learned a lot today. It was quite an, um, intense experience." She knew she wasn't expressing herself very well but she didn't have the vocabulary, nor if she were honest, the inclination to share her tumultuous feelings with the Master. Instead she asked with a nervous laugh, "So. Do I have the job?"

Donovan shook his head, smiling wryly. "Yes. Now that I'm confident you've at least had a taste of what it means to submit at the hand of another, I feel comfortable offering you the position." His tone was light, but she sensed something else simmering beneath the surface. She knew it was just a matter of time before they got to the greater issue at play here. She felt a knot in her stomach. She wasn't yet ready to admit her feelings on the matter, not even to herself.

Though she didn't know him well, she knew better than to think Donovan would let her off the hook. And sure enough, he followed with, "Now, as to that bet of ours." He let the sentence hang.

"Um," Jaime said nervously, stalling for time. "What were the terms again? You had this crazy idea I'm secretly a sub at heart, right? I think we can rule that out pretty quickly."

"Come again?" Donovan made an exaggerated expression of confusion. "That wasn't the bet, though I would argue with you, even so."

"What do you mean, you'd argue?" Jaime retorted, feeling some of her old dominant fire returning. "Subs get off on the pain. I endured it, yeah. But I definitely did not get off on it."

"Masochists get off on the pain," Donovan corrected. "But that doesn't mean it doesn't hurt, even for them. It's in how you process the pain, how you experience it. Which brings us back to the actual terms of the bet."

Jaime stiffened, waiting, aware she didn't really have a leg to stand on, and reeling from what this could possibly mean about herself. Her whole notion of herself as a Domme had been turned on its head with one session with the Master.

Donovan seemed to sense her capitulation, though she hadn't responded directly. "The terms of the bet," he continued, "were that this process would help you uncover the submissive part of your psyche that I've sensed in you from the first time I saw you watching me on the stage."

He turned to face her, capturing her gaze with his brilliant blue eyes. "Can you honestly look me in the eye right now and tell me you weren't affected, deeply affected, both physically and emotionally, by what just took place between us?"

Flames of heat moved over Jaime's cheeks and throat. She felt at once hot and cold, as if she were coming down with a fever. A part of her wanted to deny it—to refute his allegations, to pretend she hadn't felt what she'd felt, hadn't been shaken to her very core by the depth of her own reactions.

As if reading her mind, Donovan reached for her hand, taking it gently into his own. "It's not a sign of weakness, Jaime. Surely you see that? To submit takes great courage. I felt your courage today. You were afraid, but you rose above the fear. You accepted the challenge and embraced it."

Jaime found herself unable to speak, all the sassy, smartass retorts she should have had at the ready completely wiped from her repertoire. She stared mutely at the handsome Dom, wrapped in his spell as surely as a fly in a spider's web.

Finally he let go of her hand and stood, breaking the mood between them. Jaime leaned back, as if suddenly released, and breathed a long sigh of relief.

Donovan shoved his hands into his pockets, cocking his head in her direction. "I take it from your silence that you agree with me, Jaime. I have won the bet, and I fully intend that you will fulfill its terms.

Today was just a taste of what I plan to give you. Tomorrow is Sunday. I will expect you at my house no later than one o'clock. You can pack a bag if you want, but you won't need much." He flashed an evil grin, his blue eyes sparkling.

He held out a hand and Jaime took it, allowing him to help her to her feet. The sheet still wrapped around her body, she made her way to the changing room, where she'd left her clothing in a neat pile on a bench. As she pulled on her things the full import of what had just happened really began to sink in.

If today was just a taste, what in the world could she expect from two solid days and nights at the mercy of the most compelling Master she'd ever met?

"Holy cow, Jaime Anne Heller," she muttered aloud. "What the hell have you gotten yourself into now?"

# Chapter 6

Jaime stood at the front door of a small two-story white house with green shutters flanking the windows, her wheeled suitcase beside her. Excitement and uncertainty warred inside her. She must have been temporarily insane when she agreed to the bet. What the hell had she signed herself up for? If she were honest, though, brutally honest, this was about more than the bet. The Master was super sexy. He had to be attracted to her to even make such a bet in the first place. What had he said? Forty-eight hours as his personal sex slave. Not just his slave, but his *sex* slave.

A little shiver of erotic anticipation moved its way through Jaime's body at the thought of Donovan making love to her, but did she really have to go to such an extreme to get him into bed?

Okay, back to the brutal honesty. There was more going on than just sexual attraction. Whatever had happened the day before had unlocked a door hidden deep inside Jaime she hadn't even been aware was there. Though she didn't necessarily agree with Donovan's characterization of her feelings as submissive, her curiosity had certainly been piqued. Not one to turn her back on new experiences, she would push forward and learn more about this part of herself. If nothing else, it would make her a better Domme.

That didn't mean she wasn't nervous. Though it had been a very busy and exhausting Saturday night at the club, and she hadn't made it home to her apartment until after three, she'd been wide awake by ten, too keyed up by the thought of what was in store to fall back asleep. She'd waited until noon to text Donovan, not wanting to disturb him before then. He'd texted back immediately with his address, telling her to come on over when she was ready.

She looked for the doorbell. Not seeing one, she lifted the heavy brass doorknocker and let it fall against the door. As if he'd been standing just on the other side, the door swung open and there stood Donovan, his dark hair wet, his cheeks smooth from a recent shave. He had on a light blue T-shirt that made his eyes look even bluer than usual. He wore black jeans and his feet were bare.

"Hi," Jaime said, feeling suddenly shy.

"Come in, Jaime." Donovan stepped back, gesturing her inside. She found herself in a small foyer. She could see a living room through the arched opening to her right. At the back of the foyer there was a stairway that led to the second floor.

Donovan eyed Jaime's suitcase. "Whatever's in there, you won't be needing much more than your toothbrush." He flashed a wicked grin and Jaime drew in a breath, her stomach fluttering madly. Was she really going to go through with this? Was she nuts?

Donovan reached around her, shutting the front door and turning the deadbolt. His shoulder brushed hers as he moved and she caught a whiff of his scent—part soap, part aftershave, part pure male, and her nipples hardened in response. He stepped back and looked her over, his eyes sweeping her from head to toe and back again. Jaime fidgeted a little under his gaze. He hadn't told her what to wear, so she'd just dressed as she always did on her days off, in a casual knit top and jeans, sandals on her feet. She wondered if her nipples were poking through the lace of her bra and the cotton of her T-shirt but she didn't want to look down to see.

"Take off your clothes."

Though she'd heard him plainly enough, Jaime stalled for time. "I'm sorry. What?"

"Strip. I want you naked. Subs don't wear clothing in my house. Not unless they earn it." He stared at her, waiting for her to obey. She could feel the power of his will and, though her mind remained in turmoil, her fingers began to obey him. She found herself reaching for the hem of her shirt, which she grasped and lifted over her head, letting it fall to the floor. She kicked off her sandals, unzipped her jeans and pulled them down her legs.

Donovan's eyes were burning holes into her skin, and she felt it heating as if he'd lit a pilot light inside her and turned up the flame. He'd already seen her naked, and she wasn't especially shy about her body, so what was the big deal?

"Go on," he said in a quiet but firm voice. "Everything."

Swallowing, Jaime reached back and released the clasps of her bra, letting it fall forward. She dropped it onto the pile of clothes on the floor beside her. Finally she hooked her fingers into the waist of her panties and slid them off, kicking them aside.

"Donovan, I'm not sure—" Jaime began.

Donovan touched her lips with his fingertips. "Shh. No talking right now." He let his hand fall, but she could still feel the imprint of his touch on her mouth. "For the next forty-eight hours, you will only speak when answering a direct question or when I give you permission. When you do speak you will address me as Master or Sir. Got it?"

Jaime opened her mouth to protest but stopped herself. He wasn't doing anything unusual. She would have given a sub boy the same instructions at the beginning of a scene. He was just playing the role of her Dom for the next forty-eight hours. She'd agreed to the terms of the bet, so why not play along?

"Yes, Sir," she answered.

Donovan nodded. "That's better. Come have some coffee. We'll talk about my expectations for the weekend." He turned and walked through the short hallway, not looking back to see if she followed. Not knowing what else to do, Jaime did follow.

They entered a small but cheery kitchen with natural wood cabinets and windows that let in the lemony summer sunlight on either side of an old-fashioned white enamel gas range. There were two ceramic mugs, a bowl of sugar and a small creamer on a table made from polished oak, set with four white chairs with red cushions on the seats.

Donovan moved toward the counter where a coffee carafe sat on its warmer. "Cream? Sugar?" he queried as he returned to the table and poured coffee into the mugs.

The coffee smelled wonderful and Jaime's mouth watered in anticipation. "Both," she said, feeling very odd to be naked in this man's kitchen. She started to sit on one of the chairs, but Donovan stopped her.

"Subs don't sit on the furniture without permission." He pointed to a red cushion under the table that matched the ones on the chairs. "Pull that out and kneel on it. Hands clasped behind your back."

"But how will I—"

"Jaime, close your mouth!" Donovan barked. Startled, Jaime did just that. Donovan again pointed to the cushion. In a gentler tone, he said, "Kneel there.

Stop anticipating everything I do and say. Stop anticipating, period. Your job, your sole job for these two days, Jaime, is to obey and respond. Nothing else. You are not running this show. You need to let go. Of everything."

He continued to point at the cushion and Jaime found herself slowly sinking down onto it. She knew he was right. She wouldn't have tolerated one of her sub boys continuing to speak and to question her after she'd told him to be quiet. Okay, so she wasn't a sub—that was understood—but at least she could pretend to behave like one. It was, after all, just part of the scene, part of the game.

"Hands behind your back," Donovan reminded her as he sat down on the chair beside her. Jaime did as ordered, watching as he stirred cream and sugar into one mug, and just a bit of cream into the other. He lifted his mug and took a long sip. Setting the mug down, he lifted the other and leaned toward her, holding it near her mouth. The coffee-scented steam rose tantalizingly into her face.

"I'll hold it for you while you drink. You ready?" Donovan said.

The coffee was hot! What if he spilled it on her? It took every bit of self-control not to insist he let her hold the mug and drink it herself.

*Stop anticipating.*

"Yes. Yes, Sir."

Donovan placed the lip of the mug against Jaime's mouth. She opened her mouth a little and he tilted the cup carefully, letting a small bit of the hot liquid spill onto her tongue. The coffee was excellent, strong but not bitter, and Jaime savored the taste as she swallowed. He gave her several more sips and then set the mug down. As he drank from his mug he continued to look at her, his eyes moving with lazy, sensual appreciation over her bare breasts and lingering on the auburn patch between her legs.

Jaime felt suddenly self-conscious about her pubic hair. She knew the trend these days was to be completely shaven. On the BDSM porn sites she liked to visit from time to time pubic hair had become the exception, not the rule. She did groom herself, keeping her labia and bikini line smooth and soft, but she'd never wanted to shave herself bare. She'd always thought it smacked too much of submission, and Jaime Heller was nobody's sub. She might be playing one for the weekend, but she'd be damned if she'd shave for the part!

If Donovan knew what she was thinking, he made no comment. He set down his mug and lifted hers again, holding it carefully to her lips and letting her drink until the coffee was gone.

"More?" he asked.

Jaime started take shake her head no and then caught herself. "No thank you, Sir."

Donovan took another sip from his mug. Setting it down again, he turned to face her. "For the next two days you will do nothing without my permission. You won't eat, use the toilet, shower or orgasm without my express permission and direction. Though I am aware you're untrained as a sub, you are familiar with D/s protocol and as such I will expect more of you than a typical sub-in-training.

"I'm going to introduce you to an array of erotic tortures and sexual assignments as a way to gauge your response to various stimuli. I want to explore and expand on your reactions at the club yesterday. I want to understand what precisely excites you, what frightens you, what touches that inner core of submission. I know it probably seems right now like I'm just out to have fun with you, but there really is more to this. I think if you can actually connect to this basic part of yourself, it will open up a whole new vista of experience and depth in your life. You with me so far?"

"Yes, Sir."

But was she? Yes, she understood what he was saying, but he was certainly far more convinced than she was about this so-called submissive core of hers. Then she thought about the scene the day before—the feel of the flogger striking her skin like a dozen stinging fingers, the slicing cut of the cane, the rising surge of feeling that was part panic, part thrill and finally all encompassing. She'd been completely overwhelmed by the experience and while her mind had tried to reject it, she couldn't deny that some kind of fuse had been lit inside her, something that continued to sparkle and burn deep in her gut.

Donovan reached for her, his fingers grazing her cheek and trailing along her neck. Leaning forward, he moved his hand so his thumb and forefinger pressed against her throat just beneath her jaw. His hand was large and he tightened his strong fingers around her neck. Jaime gasped at the sudden, intense pressure. Her instinct was to pry his hands from her throat. She could feel her pulse beating wildly beneath his touch.

"Relax," Donovan said soothingly, though he didn't remove his hand. "My hand on your throat is just a reminder, Jaime. It's a reminder that for the next two days I own you. I will control your every move and reaction, even down to the breath you take." He squeezed a little harder and Jaime felt the pressure building behind her face. A sudden rush of panic surged through her and she whimpered.

His grip loosened just a little, though he kept his hand on her throat. He leaned closer, his face nearly touching hers. "Do you have what it takes, Jaime? Do you have the courage, the will and the desire to submit to the Master? Just your showing up today is enough for me. By your presence you confirm I won the bet and there is more to you than meets the eye.

Beyond that, I don't want you here against your will in any way. When I let go of your throat you will have a choice. You can bend down and kiss the top of my foot as a token of your willingness to submit to me wholly and without reservation for the next forty-eight hours, or you can stand up, return to the front hall and dress, and I'll see you at work on Tuesday night."

Though Donovan's hand remained on her throat, all at once her panic eased, draining away as Jaime gazed into the blue eyes of the Master. Was it her imagination or was there a quiet longing behind the stern, dominant visage? Was this only about his desire to teach her, to reach her in some way? Or was it possible this self-possessed incredibly sexy man *wanted* her as much as she wanted him?

Donovan took his hand away, his eyes still fixed on hers. Though her heart continued to pound, Jaime felt a curious sense of calm as she leaned down, touching her lips to the top of Donovan's bare foot and brushing it with a kiss.

~*~

Donovan had thought of little but Jaime's arrival since the moment she'd agreed to the terms of the bet. He couldn't wait to begin the fun, but if it wasn't truly consensual, he wasn't interested. When she kissed his foot, Donovan let out a breath he hadn't realized he'd been holding. This was it. The training would now begin.

"Stand up."

Jaime rose from the cushion. Donovan stood too, reaching into the back pocket of his jeans. He held out four strips of black leather, each about six inches long with slits cut at intervals into them, and a silver clip sewn on the outside of each. They were new, purchased just for Jaime. From his other pocket he withdrew a handful of clips.

"Hold out your wrists," he said. "You'll wear these cuffs for the duration of your stay here, except when you bathe." She held out her wrists and Donovan closed the cuffs around them one at a time, pushing the D ring through a slit and clipping it in place.

"Now your ankles." Donovan sat on a chair and pointed to his knee. "Left foot first."

Her feet were pretty, with high arches and long, straight toes. Her toenails, like her fingernails, were painted pearly pink. He secured the ankle cuffs, letting his fingers slide over the smooth skin of her muscular calf. He wanted to fuck her, but he recognized there was a lot he wanted to accomplish and that Jaime would need to achieve before she merited the gift of her Master's cock.

Since that first time he'd seen her at one of his shows, he'd seen the burning embers of her submission hidden beneath the confidant swagger of her dominance. He believed he could be the one to fan those embers into flames of pure passion.

What might happen beyond that?

Donovan gave an internal shrug. Let the future take care of itself. He was interested in the *now*. He looked into Jaime's eyes, which were wide, the pupils dilated. Her cheeks were gently flushed, her nipples standing at pert attention. A sudden fantasy of pushing her back against the kitchen table and fucking her then and there roared through his head like a freight train. He angled away from Jaime so she wouldn't see the bulge of his erection as he pushed the image down.

Donovan moved toward a drawer where he kept various toys and pulled out a metal dog leash. Returning to Jaime, he said, "Put your wrists together." He clipped the cuffs together and then attached the leash to the clips. Taking the leather handle of the leash, he tugged gently. "Let's go. I'll show you around."

He led her out of the kitchen, pleased that she followed docilely. They went up the stairs, Jaime behind him by a few steps, her wrists held out before her. He led her first into the bedroom. He watched her take in the cuffs hanging from the corners of the four-poster bed, and the whips displayed on the wall above the bed.

"Oh," Jaime said softly.

Donovan tugged at her leash to pull her from the room. "Meanwhile, let me show you my home dungeon. You'll be spending a lot of time in there."

He led her along the hallway to the second bedroom, which he'd converted into a fully equipped BDSM playroom. His cock hardened as he visualized this lovely young woman tethered in the black rubber spider's web, or bent over the spanking horse, or hung suspended from the ceiling beams, her back and ass striped by the lash, her bare chest heaving in anticipation of more to come.

He led Jaime into the center of the room and removed the leash from her wrists, though he left them clipped together. He allowed her a little time to take in the space. As a Domme herself and active in the scene, he knew he didn't have to explain the purpose of the equipment and toys. He couldn't wait to get started.

Crossing to the sofa he'd installed against one of the walls, Donovan sat. "Jaime, your training begins now. You've committed to staying, and to doing your best to obey and to learn. We could start with a typical warm up session, not all that different from what you experienced yesterday at the club. Fact is," he continued, "I'm feeling a little self-indulgent at the moment, and we're going to start with a good, old-fashioned spanking. Get over here and lie on my lap."

He rubbed his palms together in eager anticipation as the girl approached. He could see the hesitation in her eyes and feel her resistance. To her credit she came to him. He helped her into position as she lay awkwardly over his knees. He wished suddenly he was naked so he could feel skin on skin while he spanked her.

*Not yet*, he told himself. *Not yet.*

He felt a tremor move through her body as he stroked her back and ass. He cupped her rounded cheeks, noting one faint mark that still lingered from the whipping the day before. He would add more marks, many more, before the two days were over.

He thought of other women he'd marked over the years, some just casual play partners, others he'd had a serious relationship with, though those never lasted too long. All of them, to a one, had loved to go to the mirror after an especially intense session and twist back to see the marks of courage he'd painted on their flesh.

Would Jaime feel the same way? Or was she only going through this experience because she was stubborn as a mule and determined to prove she could do it? Time would tell, he supposed. For now all he needed to do was give this dominant sub girl a spanking she wouldn't soon forget.

"I want you to relax. No squirming. It's okay if you make noise, but don't ask me to stop. I'll stop when I decide." He paused, stroking the satin of her skin. "Are you ready?"

She didn't answer immediately. Donovan could feel the tension she was holding in her body. If she were at all trained, he would have punished her for this hesitation in responding to a direct question, but as it was he just waited. He continued to stroke her, moving his palms over her ass and the backs of her thighs. He let his hands trail along her sides, pressing them against the soft, yielding curve of her breasts.

"Yes, Sir," she finally whispered. "I'm ready."

# Chapter 7

For the first time in years, Jaime thought of Billy, a college boyfriend. He'd called her his kinky partner in crime, as the two of them had explored budding BDSM fantasies in the privacy of his studio apartment. Billy was mostly masochistic, though still finding his way, while Jaime was just beginning to acknowledge her dominant impulses. Back then they didn't have any of the BDSM toys she'd come to acquire over the years, though Billy was inventive with his use of wooden spoons and clothesline.

Mostly, though, they'd done just what Donovan was doing now. Spanking had been their foreplay of choice, and Jaime had even been on the receiving end a time or two. Though it had been little more than a game, Jaime had thought them sophisticated and wild at the time. The spankings had never been especially hard. It had been more about forbidden fun and pushing the envelope of acceptable behavior. D/s or the concept of erotic suffering had never really entered into it.

But Billy had been a boy, and Donovan was every inch a man. Jaime could feel the hard muscles of his thigh against her stomach. She could feel his power and his absolute control of the situation. She could feel her own lack of control, her wrists cuffed in front of her as she lay naked on his lap.

She couldn't deny his hands felt wonderful moving over her body, massaging away her tension with his big, calloused palms and fingertips. As he touched the sides of her breasts, she had to stifle the impulse to moan, to roll over and reach for him.

"What's your safeword?" Donovan asked.

"I don't have one. I'm a Domme," Jaime found herself retorting.

"Then I'll give you one. Apple. I don't expect you'll need it, but if for some reason you can't tolerate what is happening at any time over the course of the next two days, you can use it. You understand it's a total scene stopper, right? You use it, you better sure as hell mean it."

"Yes, yes, of course I understand," Jaime replied, trying to keep the testiness out of her voice. He had stopped touching her while he delivered his little lecture. She wanted his hands back on her body, stroking her breasts and smoothing her back. At the same time, his words disquieted her. A safeword! Would things really get that intense? *Apple,* she said silently, committing it to memory.

"Okay, then. Time for your spanking."

Like the pro he was, Donovan started with an easy, steady smack, warming her skin in a lightly stinging caress. Soon, however, his palm landed harder, the sound of contact cracking in the air. Jaime was determined to remain still. She would show the Master just how courageous and obedient she could be, whether or not there was anything to his assertion she was secretly submissive.

Suddenly the sting intensified. He wasn't hitting her any harder, but he'd changed the shape of his hand and now each cupped blow landed with painful precision. Though she'd planned to stay quiet, an "Ah!" of pain pushed its way out of her mouth.

The next several blows hurt even more, and Jaime felt sweat prickling beneath her arms and on her forehead. She grunted, clenching her fists as if this could somehow help her handle the pain.

"Relax," Donovan instructed from above. "When you tense, you bunch your muscles and that compresses the nerve endings and intensifies the pain. That's not submission, Jaime. It's resistance. It's disobedience. Relax. Breathe. Flow with the pain. It's a river. Let it take you."

*Easy for you to say.* Jaime clenched her teeth to keep from snarling this at him. Still, she tried to do as he said, willing her muscles to unclench and drawing in a deep breath of air. Still his palm crashed against her, hard as wood against her throbbing cheeks.

She jumped when she felt the fingers of his other hand brush along the back of her thigh. They moved inward, pushing her legs apart and for a second Jaime forgot the stinging pain of the spanking. She gasped as his fingers touched her sex, tickling along her outer labia. She groaned as one digit slid its way into her opening. She could feel the clench of her muscles around the finger and her clit pulsed.

He continued to spank her as hard as or perhaps harder than before, but it was suddenly easier to bear, juxtaposed against the deep and arousing pleasure of his finger moving like a small, hard cock inside her. Again she groaned, but then grunted with pain as his palm crashed hard against her.

Keeping one finger inside her, he maneuvered until she felt a fingertip graze her swollen clit. In spite of herself, Jaime's pelvis twitched, shifting to increase the pressure of his touch. She heard him chuckle softly over her head as his fingers were withdrawn from her sex. "Stay still, randy girl. You're not in control here."

Embarrassed, she stilled, though her clit throbbed. He spanked her without the sweet distraction of his other hand. It fucking *hurt*! If her hands hadn't been cuffed in front of her, she would have put them over her ass to shield herself from the blows. As it was, she had no choice but to endure the spanking, whimpering and again squirming beneath his hard touch despite his admonition to stay still.

When his fingers finally slid back between her legs, Jaime again groaned her approval. Forgetting herself, she writhed against his hand. It felt so good. This time he slid two fingers inside her. Jaime wanted more. She wanted to be fucked. She *needed* to be fucked.

Again that soft, confident laugh. Jaime would have bristled but she was too busy reacting to the steady, stinging blows of his hard palm intertwining with the intense, perfect thrust of his fingers inside her and the hot stroke of a fingertip at her clit. If only he would stop hitting her, damn it, then she could come!

The blows intensified and Jaime lost her sexual rhythm. *Fuck, it hurts. It hurts, it hurts, it hurts.* "No!" she cried, the word ripped from her mouth. "I can't!"

Donovan didn't reply. He kept right on smacking her, his other hand still buried between her legs. Finally exhaustion forced the tension from her muscles and Jaime found her fingers and toes uncurling, her body sinking heavily against Donovan's legs.

"That's it," Donovan murmured encouragingly. "You're getting there."

His fingers moved at her sex, which felt swollen and very wet. Jaime moaned and sighed, both from pleasure at his expert touch and relief that the spanking had become easier to bear. Intellectually she recognized her nerve endings were probably deadening from the repeated blows, though he continued to hit her as hard as before. But was that all it was?

Whatever was happening, there was no question that she was going to come. His touch was the perfect combination of gentleness and intensity. She could feel the rising tremble in her loins and hear her own steady, uncontrolled moaning, made breathy as she panted through the pain of the spanking.

"Oh god, oh god," she heard herself gasping.

His palm struck her mercilessly, while his fingers remained relentlessly perfect inside her. "You will ask permission to come." He spoke so calmly while she writhed and panted on his lap, barely able to process his words, her brain short-circuiting against the steady onslaught of pleasure and pain.

Like a wave, her orgasm rose inside her, lifting her out of herself. She tried to speak, to ask, to beg. "Please, can I, oh god, oh fuck, oh..."

"Yes."

The wave crashed, sending her tumbling head over feet, caught in its vortex, sucked down into the most intense, all-encompassing orgasm she'd ever experienced in her life. Dimly she heard the sound of someone keening and realized it was she. Her heart was smashing through her chest as she twisted and flailed on Donovan's lap, her body lifted into an arc of nearly unbearable pleasure.

Finally she collapsed, completely spent, her body bathed in sweat, her heart thumping steadily against Donovan's legs. She felt him release the clips that held her wrists cuffs together, and then his arms moved beneath her, lifting and turning her until she was cradled against him, her cheek resting on his chest.

She wasn't sure how long she lay in his arms, her eyes closed, not quite conscious. Her mind felt blank, but it was a peaceful emptiness, like drifting in a vast, calm ocean, warm sun bathing her body, suspended in utter, perfect serenity.

When she finally opened her eyes, he was looking down at her as if memorizing the planes and angles of her face. When he saw her eyes were open, he smiled, a small, soft smile without a trace of arrogance. Still bathed in the afterglow of the experience, Jaime found herself smiling back.

"Kiss me," she whispered and then parted her lips, lifting her chin in invitation.

Donovan leaned down, touching his lips to hers. They kissed lightly at first. She closed her eyes, enjoying the sensation of his mouth on hers. Then his kiss deepened, his tongue entering her mouth as he pulled her close.

She wrapped her arms around his neck, letting her tongue glide past his. This was good. It felt right. She could feel the hard press of his erection against her hip. He wanted her. He would make love to her now. Her cunt throbbed. In spite of the recent powerful orgasm, she was ready for him. She longed to feel his cock filling her.

She pulled away from his kiss long enough to whisper in his ear, "I want to fuck you." She pushed at his shoulders, trying to shove him onto his back, the scenario already full-blown in her mind. She would undo his belt, pull the zipper of his fly open, drag the denim from his legs. Triumphantly she would grasp his erect shaft and bend down to lick away the drop of pre-come at its tip. Then she would straddle him, locking eyes as she eased herself onto him.

She wanted, she suddenly realized, to realign the balance of power. She wanted to make him mad with passion for her—to control his lust as she moved over him, riding him like a stallion, leading him by the rein of her feminine power to an orgasm that would leave him weak with desire and totally in her command.

"You do, huh?" Donovan grinned, remaining immobile against her attempts to move him into a supine position. Instead he closed his arms more firmly around her and stood, lifting her into the air. He set her unceremoniously on her ass on the floor and pointed to his bare foot.

"That's something you're a long way from earning. Now, kneel properly and thank me for the spanking and the orgasm. It'll be the last one for a while. We're going to move on now to a little basic training."

Jaime felt the heat flooding into her face. A dozen retorts rose to her lips. Who the fuck did he think he was! He was smiling down at her with a shit-eating grin, his eyebrows lifting as if to say, *What, you have a problem with that?*

Then she remembered herself, and the bet, and what she had signed on for. If she balked now, he would win, or more precisely, she would lose. She had promised herself to approach this weekend with an open mind. She had been letting her cunt get in the way of rational thinking. If a sub had told her he wanted to fuck her while they were in the middle of training, she would have laughed in his face. At least Donovan hadn't done that!

Blowing out a breath, Jaime forced herself into position on her knees and leaned forward. Her ass still smarted from the spanking but embarrassment at his refusal had snuffed her lust, leaving only chagrin. Still, she knew the drill. Good little sub girls did what they were told. It was only for two days. Piece of cake.

She kissed the top of his foot. "Thank you, Sir."

~*~

"One key feature of submissive behavior is putting aside your pride. Your role as a submissive is to serve, to honor and obey your Master without hesitation and without concern for your own pleasure or pride. It's not enough just to go through the motions. A true submissive puts her Master before herself. Her sense of ego satisfaction is derived from pleasing and obeying her Master."

They stood in the playroom facing one another. Donovan could almost hear Jaime's decidedly unsubmissive thoughts at the assertion that this somehow applied to her. He watched the play of emotions move over her face, but to her credit, she kept her mouth shut. And what a lovely mouth it was, the lower lip full, protruding slightly as she listened. He wanted to bite it. He wanted to kiss her again. He wanted to fuck her. Oh god, he wanted that.

And she wanted to fuck him. Of course she did, after what he'd done to her. He wasn't egocentric enough to think she really wanted him, Donovan the man. No, what she'd been reacting to was Donovan, the Master, and feelings he'd been able to pull from her during the spanking/titillation exercise. Which was in itself a good thing—if she was as hardcore a dominant as she tried to maintain, no way could she have come like that during a spanking. The fact that she then wanted to have sex was even more proof she was turned on by what had occurred, whether or not she was ready to admit it.

Her approach, however, had been decidedly dominant when she tried to push him over, her expression filled with masterful intention. It was that behavior he was determined to tame. Jaime was still operating off her feminine charms, which he had to admit were considerable. His goal by the end of the two days was to have her naked, not only literally, but metaphorically. He would show her the naked beauty and power of submission.

The fetch exercise would be a good place to start chipping away at her dominant armor. He held out the small red rubber ball. "Get on your hands and knees. I'm going to toss this ball and you will crawl to wherever it lands and retrieve it with your mouth. No hands. Bring it back to me and place it at my feet."

Jaime's brow furrowed, her mouth pulling down into a frown. Donovan moved quickly to close the space between them. He slapped her right cheek. Jaime gasped, bringing her hand to her face, her eyes wide with shock.

"There are different forms of disobedience, as you well know," Donovan said firmly. "One important aspect of control, young lady, is learning to control your expression. You're here right now as my sub, don't forget. If you don't like something I tell you, or you have a real concern about being able to follow an order, you may ask for permission to speak. I will listen to your concerns and make my decision. You will *not* scrunch up your face like some bratty kid. Is that understood?"

Her eyes flashed, but Donovan stared her down, pleased when the fire went out of them and her brow smoothed. "Yes, Sir," she said softly.

He pointed again to the carpet. "On your hands and knees." He waited for her to obey. Then he tossed the ball lightly across the floor. Jaime didn't move, as if waiting for Donovan to tell her he was kidding. He crossed his arms over his chest. He would give her five seconds, and then he would punish her.

*One. Two. Three. Four.*

She began to crawl in the direction of the ball. Donovan admired the sway of her ass as she headed toward the corner where the ball had rolled. She bent down, biting the small ball and turning back toward him. Despite his admonition to control her features, he could see the fury in her face.

They would have to work on that.

She returned to him and lowered her head, dropping the ball beside his left foot. Donovan reached down to retrieve it and tossed it again. Again the mutinous stare, but this time she began to crawl after only two seconds. She brought the ball back and again he tossed it. With a little sigh of impatience, she again crawled in the direction of the ball. This time it had rolled beneath the spanking sawhorse and Jaime had to maneuver carefully to get the ball from between the legs of the horse but she managed.

When she dropped the ball once more at his feet, she made a show of spitting out bits of carpet fuzz. Donovan watched, tolerantly amused. He picked up the ball, wet from her saliva, and wiped it against his thigh. He moved toward the whip rack and withdrew a long-handled riding crop.

"You're going through the motions," he observed, "but you're still exhibiting far too much pride. You move too slowly and you think too much. Let's try this again with a little help from the crop."

He tossed the ball again and this time when she began to crawl he walked behind her, smacking her ass and thighs with the crop. "Faster," he admonished. "Move!"

She yelped but sped up, moving quickly over the carpet on her hands and knees. She bent for the ball, her ass lifting alluringly into the air as she did so. He could see the pucker of her little asshole and his cock hardened at the thought of penetrating it. Was she an anal virgin? Not that it mattered.

She twisted back, the ball in her mouth. She dropped it by his feet, looking hopefully up at him. He retrieved the ball and tossed it again, and her hopeful look slid away, replaced again with a bratty expression. Silly girl. She was her own worst enemy.

He cropped her ass as she scurried along after the ball, which had rolled to the sofa, stopping just at its edge. "Be careful," he warned. "If it rolls under there you won't be able to get it. If you can't retrieve the ball, I'll have to punish you."

"But—" she began to protest, before catching herself. She pressed her lips together. Donovan waited, watching her. She shifted, moving carefully as she lowered her mouth to the ball. It started to roll but she managed to get hold of it. Again she turned toward him, her expression triumphant.

Donovan pointed to the ground at his feet. She dropped the ball. He tossed it again. It was clear she was getting fatigued, but she was young and strong, and he prodded her along with the crop, forcing her to retrieve the ball again and again until all the mutinous fire had been extinguished from her expression and she sought only to obey.

Finally Donovan took the ball from between her teeth before she could drop it. "Good girl," he said, patting her head. "You deserve a treat. Get up on your haunches and lift your arms like this." Donovan demonstrated, bending his arms at the elbows and holding his hands up in front of his chest like an eager puppy begging for a bone.

Jaime didn't move. She flushed, two red spots appearing like spots of rouge on her cheeks while her neck turned red. Donovan watched, fascinated at her level of resistance. He wasn't used to dealing with someone like this. She was indeed a challenge.

"Pride," he reminded her softly. Finally she sat back on her haunches and slowly lifted her arms into position. Donovan nodded his approval. "Better," he said. "You're like a little doggie waiting for her bone." The flush deepened, but she managed to maintain her puppy pose.

Donovan left her there while he went to the treat drawer. He took out a small piece of Belgian chocolate from its gold foil wrapper and returned to her. "You like chocolate?" He held out the piece of candy.

"Yes, Sir."

"Open your mouth and stick out your tongue."

She did as she was told. Donovan had a sudden erotically-charged fantasy of pulling out his aching cock and placing it there instead of the chocolate. He would have loved to hold her head in his hands as he eased his girth between her lips, pushing forward until his cock touched the back of her throat. Yes, he would do that. He would definitely do that, and soon. But first, the good little puppy had earned her chocolate treat.

He leaned down and placed the bit of confection on her pretty pink tongue and then patted her head. "Good girl," he said, ignoring the sudden, reignited flash of defiance in her pretty green eyes.

They would work on that. Oh yes, they would.

# Chapter 8

At lunch Donovan insisted on feeding Jaime, who knelt on the cushion at his feet. "It's time to ratchet up the intensity, Jaime. After all, we only have a day and a half left."

Jaime pondered this as she chewed. The time so far had already been pretty damn intense as far as she was concerned. But he hadn't asked for her input, and she offered none. She had come very close to outright refusing to crawl around like a dog, even though intellectually she understood the purpose of the exercise.

The spanking had been something else, more powerful and erotically charged than she'd expected, and the orgasm had been without question the most intense one of her life. Was that because of the spanking, or in spite of it? She honestly didn't know.

After lunch Donovan led her back upstairs, this time to the master bedroom. "You need to pee?" he asked her.

Jaime nodded, and then caught herself and added aloud, "Yes, Sir."

Donovan led her into the bathroom. She stood there waiting for him to leave the room. Instead he leaned against the counter, watching her in that amused, exasperating way she was coming to recognize as his *go on, I dare you to refuse me* look.

Biting back a sigh, Jaime lowered herself to the toilet and emptied her bladder. She kept her face averted from Donovan while she peed, though she could feel his eyes on her. When she was done and washing her hands, Donovan stepped to the toilet, lifted the lid, extracted his cock from his jeans and peed noisily into the bowl without the slightest trace of self-consciousness. It was easier for men, Jaime decided. They were used to peeing in public at urinals. It was no big deal to them.

They went back into the bedroom. "Get on the bed," Donovan instructed. Now this was more like it. Bed equaled sex, right? Jaime was definitely ready for some hot, sweaty sex with this sexy man. She'd certainly *earned* it, hadn't she?

But Donovan wasn't pulling off his shirt and unzipping his jeans. Instead, he opened the drawer of the night table and pulled out several coils of ropes and a shrink wrapped item. Setting the rope down on the bed beside her, Donovan stripped off the sterile wrapping to reveal a large stainless steel hook with a metal loop on one end, and two stainless steel balls like a tiny snowman welded to the curved end of the hook, one the size of a ping pong ball, the other the size of a golf ball.

"You know what this is?" Donovan held the ominous-looking device up for Jaime's inspection.

She swallowed hard. "Yes, Sir," she managed. She'd seen these on porn sites, but holy crap, he wasn't actually going to use that on *her*, was he?

"Tell me," the Master instructed. "Tell me in your own words what this is."

"It's an anal hook, Sir. Except there're two balls at the end?"

"That's right. I like this better than a single ball. It goes deeper into the anus than a single ball. And this ring loop is handy for rope. Too bad your hair isn't long enough. If it was, I would use your hair to hold the hook in place. As it is, we'll just use the rope."

He pointed toward the ceiling and Jaime followed his gaze to a large eyebolt, one of several anchored into the ceiling above the bed. How many other women had been the subject, or should she say the object, of his erotic training? How many of them had been his lover as well as his sub?

She looked again at the anal hook and felt her ass cheeks clenching. Though she had experienced anal sex before, she had an aversion to what she thought of as "foreign objects" being put inside of her orifices, especially her ass. She watched with rising trepidation as Donovan pulled a tube of lubricant from the drawer.

"Permission to speak, Sir?" she ventured.

Donovan turned to her. "Of course."

"I'm not sure… I mean, I don't like things in my ass." Jaime felt herself blushing but pushed on. "You know, things, foreign objects. It makes me nervous. Especially something like that, you know? It seems kind of dangerous. I'm not comfortable with it."

Donovan looked at her thoughtfully. "Okay. I hear you."

Jaime felt a rush of relief, but this gave way to confusion as Donovan took a hank of rope and began to loop it through the ring on the end of the anal hook. "What're you doing?" Jaime blurted. "I just said I don't like that. It makes me nervous."

Donovan nodded calmly, though he didn't stop what he was doing. "Yes. I heard you say that. I understand."

"So…?" Jaime let the question hang. What was going on?

"So, that's fine. You have registered your discomfort with this exercise. I have heard you and taken that into consideration. Now I want you to get on your hands and knees on the end of the bed, ass out. I'm going to insert this double-balled anal hook into that pretty ass of yours, and then I'm going to tie the other end with this rope to the hook in the ceiling. We'll use a thinner cane this time, one that marks the skin more easily."

Apparently seeing the look that must have been on Jaime's face, Donovan grinned and shook his head. "Don't worry. The three bywords are still at play here. The way I'm going to position you will not put you in danger. The hook is really just there to encourage you to stay still."

"But..." Jaime bleated, dumbstruck. Was he serious? Jaime's heart had kicked into overdrive. Was this the time to use her safeword?

Donovan set the hook and rope down and sat on the bed next to Jaime. He took her face into his hands and peered into her soul with his deep blue eyes. "Stop fighting me, Jaime. Let me take you to a new place. Trust me." Jaime felt the panicked pounding of her heart easing as she stared into his eyes. She wanted to trust him. She wanted to give this a chance.

"But I'm scared," she found herself saying.

"I understand." Donovan nodded. "Fear in and of itself is not a bad thing. It can heighten an erotic experience, especially for someone like you."

*Someone like you...*

Jaime no longer knew what this meant. He seemed so sure, yet still she resisted. *Trust me.* Slowly she nodded. She would try. She always had her safeword if things got too scary or too intense to handle. "Okay. Okay, Sir," she finally agreed.

Donovan grinned. "Glad I have your permission, sub girl. Now, get on your hands and knees like I told you. Go on, move." He stood, retrieving the hook and rope while Jaime moved into position on the end of the bed, her heart again kicking into gear.

She jerked forward when the cold, lubricated metal ball touched her sphincter. "Relax," Donovan soothed. "The first ball is so small you'll hardly feel it. We'll take it nice and slow, as slow as you need." He pushed the ball against her puckered entrance, his touch light but steady. Jaime squealed as the ball pressed past the ring of muscle, not so much from pain, but from fear.

Once it was in, Donovan gave her a minute to adjust. Then he said, "Okay, ball two now. You'll feel this one more. Just relax. Let yourself enter a submissive state of mind. Open your body and your spirit to what I'm giving you."

Jaime's breath came shallow and fast, her gut lurching with rising panic. She didn't know how to relax, not with this thing being shoved into her! She had no idea how to open her body, much less her spirit.

*Apple.*

That was all she had to do—just say the word and the action would cease. *You can do it. Listen to him. Relax.* Jaime had no idea where this small but insistent voice in her head came from, but she closed her mouth, pressing her lips together to keep from saying the safeword.

Donovan pushed at the gooey metal ball again and suddenly it felt as if Jaime's ass was being split open. She screamed at the sudden, biting pain and then— And then, nothing. It didn't hurt anymore. She nearly laughed with relief.

"Good job," Donovan enthused. "It's all the way in. Jesus, you look hot. Let me get the rope secured and then I'll show you." He climbed onto the mattress and stood. He reached up, knotting the rope that was tied to the anal hook over the eyebolt in the ceiling. Jaime could feel the tension of the rope against the hook now buried in her ass. This was far more effective than tying her down to the bed, she realized. She didn't dare move, no matter what happened.

Donovan climbed off the bed and went into the walk-in closet on the side of the room. He came out holding a large mirror on a stand, which he placed beside the bed, tilting it until Jaime got a view of herself that made her gasp. The large stainless steel hook emerged from between her ass cheeks as if she were a side of beef suspended by the hook and rope. It looked, she realized, a lot scarier than it felt.

Donovan left the mirror where it was. He showed Jaime the cane he was going to use. It was shorter and thinner than the one he'd used at the club and would, she knew, pack a stronger, whippier sting. "Let's make this a little more interesting," Donovan said, again reaching into the drawer beside the bed. This time he extracted another shrink-wrapped package, which Jaime saw was a pink dildo with a small protrusion near the bottom she recognized as a clit tickler.

Donovan squirted lubricant onto the head of the vibrator and stepped behind Jaime. She could see him in the mirror, at least his lower half, as he placed the head of the vibrator between her legs. She felt the phallus being pushed into her cunt—another foreign object—but certainly easier to tolerate than the anal hook. She could feel the clit tickler nestling snugly between her labia. The fullness inside her ass and pussy were almost overwhelming. Yet at the same time, there was a certain erotic comfort to the fullness that surprised her.

Donovan turned the base of the vibrator and it whirred to life inside of her, the clit tickler vibrating along with the rest of it. It made the metal balls buried in her ass vibrate too and as odd as it was to admit it, it felt kind of nice.

"You have permission in advance to come. You don't have to ask during this exercise," Donovan informed her. As if she'd be able to come while being caned, with a freaking anal hook buried in her ass!

Jaime glanced at herself in the mirror, unable to stop staring at the huge silver hook emerging from her ass, tied with rope that hung at a forty-five degree angle to the ceiling. There was enough give in the rope to allow her some movement, but if she fell forward or jerked too hard, what would happen inside her? She shuddered at the thought, and reminded herself all she had to do was stay in position and she would be fine.

"You good, Jaime? Everything okay?"

*Is that a trick question?* she wanted to quip. Would *he* be okay with an anal hook shoved up his ass? Jaime forced herself to focus on the question in the spirit in which it was intended. She, too, checked with her subs once she had them in whatever position they would stay in for the duration of a session. He was only practicing proper D/s safety protocol.

"Yes, Sir," she replied, just as properly. If things got out of hand, she'd just use her safeword. Donovan was a pro. He would stop the action instantly, she knew.

He started the caning lightly, the same as he'd done the day before at the club. It hurt more from the outset though, the sting more focused and pronounced. When the first real stroke landed Jaime jerked reflexively, which caused the hook buried in her ass to tug inside her. Was that dangerous? In spite of his assurances, she didn't want to find out the hard way, and made a mental note to stay as still as possible.

She glanced sidelong again at the mirror. Her breasts swayed, the nipples fully erect at the tips, her back arched, her ass thrust out, the stainless steel hook rising lewdly from between her cheeks. She couldn't see the upper half of Donovan's body in the mirror, but she could see his hand, and the cane as it whipped over her skin.

The cane stung like a line of angry bees along her ass and thighs. Jaime twitched with each painful stroke, but didn't dare move too much. The vibrator whirring inside her was also beginning to do its work, along with the tickler that was teasing her engorged clit. The mixture of pleasure and pain was confusing to her body, though her mind understood the purpose of the exercise. The Master was trying to blend the two for her, to show her that woven together they could be more powerful than either sensation alone.

She stopped thinking when the cane struck her body just where her ass met her thighs. A line of fire ripped its way over her flesh and she gasped in stunned pain. Before she could even form words of protest, another line of fire seared over her skin, just above the first one. She jerked and screamed but instead of stopping, Donovan caned her again and again and again. Jaime began to tremble, even while she knew she had to remain in position on her hands and knees, or risk jerking the anal hook from her body.

*Apple. You can say it.*

But she didn't say it. She wasn't sure why. Her cunt was throbbing, her clit exploding in a series of mini climaxes that distracted her, at least momentarily, from the relentless cut of the cane. She could hear the whipping, whooshing sound of the cane as it hurtled through the air in the split second before it landed against her skin.

She felt Donovan doing something to the vibrator, and suddenly it shifted to a higher level of vibration that transferred itself across the thin membrane that separated her vaginal and anal canals, and caused the metal balls in her ass to vibrate as well. Still the cane came crashing down in a steady blaze of fire, the whoosh of the cane now instantly followed by her agonized cries of pain.

At the same time the cane was welting her skin, the vibrator continued its work, lifting her into a fully realized and powerful orgasm. She jerked and felt the tension of the hook inside her, but she was unable to control her shuddering. The cane landed again and again on her flayed skin. Hot tears wet her lashes and blurred her sight as they fell like raindrops to the sheet beneath her.

She felt as if she were at the top of a cliff, panic about to propel her over the edge. She would fall, screaming and flailing, unable to break the fall, unable to save herself...

"I can't, I can't, I can't, I can't..." She heard herself whispering these words over and over, though it just sounded like an inarticulate muttering, a hiss of sound, interspersed with cries of pain and gasps of pleasure.

But Donovan somehow understood the words, because, dimly over the roar of her pounding heart and the steady whoosh of the cane, she heard him say, "You *can*. You *are*. You're *amazing*, Jaime. You're almost there. Let go, baby. Let it all go. This is what you were born for."

The cane continued to strike her skin, and it hurt just as much as it had a second before. The vibrator continued to tease and titillate her cunt and ass until she thought she was going to pass out from the stimulation. Her tears continued to fall and her body continued to shudder and tremble. But the panic that had a moment before threatened to engulf her dissipated somewhat beneath Donovan's encouraging words.

She was crying full out now, noisy, gasping sobs wrenched from somewhere deep inside her. She was again on the edge of the cliff, too exhausted now, and too overwhelmed to resist any longer. Closing her eyes, she leaned forward and let herself…slip…over the edge…

But instead of hurtling and tumbling down into her panic, she found herself floating, soaring like a bird wheeling high overhead. She was still inside her body—she could still feel the cane and the vibrator and the anal hook—but the pain was gone. Or rather, it had somehow transmuted into something different. Something not only bearable, but rather, something sublime. Something to be sought, embraced, taken deep inside.

"Yes," she breathed, though no sound came from her. It didn't matter. She continued to soar on the wind, a sense of the most pure and profound peace she'd ever experienced in her life settling over her like grace itself.

Vaguely she became aware of the vibrator being turned off and gently pulled from her body. And then the anal hook was removed, slipping painlessly from her ass. She remained on her hands and knees, actually unable to move, still caught in the trance that had lifted her out of herself so completely. She didn't want to come back—she wanted to stay in this quiet, unearthly place of pure serenity.

She felt Donovan settle beside her on the bed. She didn't resist him as he pulled her down onto her side. She was still crying, she realized, though now it was just tears coursing down her cheeks and sliding into her hair. He pulled her gently into his arms, spooning her from behind and wrapping his arms around her torso.

"I've got you," he whispered into her ear as her heavy eyelids closed. "You're safe in my arms. Take as long as you need to."

She wanted to answer, to thank him for the amazing session, to wonder aloud what had happened to her and what it was she was experiencing, but she had lost the capacity to speak. She couldn't even move or open her eyes, though she wasn't asleep, not by any stretch. He seemed to sense this, and he didn't press her, or try to make her talk. He just held her and his presence was warm and comforting as she slowly floated back into herself.

Then an overwhelming fatigue moved through her, as if she'd run three marathons in a row, or climbed the highest mountain in the world. She had come back into herself, she realized with a pang—she would have liked to stay wherever he'd taken her forever, but of course that wasn't possible. The deep feeling of wellbeing had stayed with her, however, and she gave in to the fatigue, letting the heaviness move through her limbs. She sighed, a deep, satisfied sigh and snuggled back against Donovan's warm, strong body as he held her in his arms.

She wanted to tell Donovan about what she'd experienced. Did he have any idea what had happened? She needed to share this amazing thing with someone. She tried to speak, but only managed to say, "Mmmm…"

And then she was asleep.

# Chapter 9

There was a softness to Jaime's features as she stared up at Donovan from her cushion on the floor beside the table. Her large green eyes were shining with a submissive glow. The sassy smirk that had lifted her pretty lips so often at the club was nowhere in evidence. Amazing what an anal hook and a cane could do, Donovan thought with an inward grin.

He'd let her nap while he'd prepared their dinner, proud he'd resisted the very strong temptation to get naked and take the girl then and there, the bet and the training be damned. He had every right to fuck her, of course. That had been part of the agreement, but he wanted to make the submission more real for her — more intense. And that meant keeping tight rein on his own sexual impulses in order to give her a more powerful experience. She had to earn his cock with erotic suffering and sacrifice. It would be the grand finale of the weekend.

He fed her another bite of pork chop, followed by a bit of roasted potatoes and then held the glass of red wine to her lips, careful not to spill its contents as she sipped. In spite of his resolve, his cock was hard as a bar of iron as he drank in the sight of the naked beauty on her knees. As much to distract himself as anything, he said, "I haven't forgotten the way you were watching from the edge of the crowd when I did the hot wax scene with Linda. Your expression was priceless—part fear, part longing. I think we'll recreate that scene after dinner, wax, whip and all."

"Oh!" Jaime said, her eyes widening, her hand moving to cover her pubic mound. Donovan let his eyes linger pointedly on her hand. When she didn't move it, he frowned.

"Are you forgetting yourself? You know better than that. Subs don't cover their bodies. Are you looking for punishment?"

With obvious reluctance, Jaime let her hand fall away. "It's just that…" she began and then trailed off.

"Just what? You have an issue with hot wax?"

"No, it's not that. Not exactly. It's just…" Again she failed to complete her sentence.

Donovan reached down, placing his hand under her chin and forcing it gently upward as he looked into her eyes. "Jaime. Tell me what it is that's bothering you."

He suppressed a smile as a rosy blush moved over her cheeks, her small chin still cupped in his palm as he waited for her to continue. Finally she said, "It's just that, well, you know, I'm not shaven. Dried wax and pubic hair can be something of a mess."

"Agreed." Donovan nodded, releasing her. He took a long drink from his wine and added casually, "Much harder to whip off too." Jaime bit her lip and wrapped her arms protectively around her body at this statement, no doubt remembering the flick of the whip against Linda's wax-covered body and imagining herself in Linda's place.

"Position," Donovan reminded Jaime, pleased that she dropped her arms, though her lower lip remained caught in her teeth. "There is a solution, of course." When Jaime didn't answer, he continued. "We can make you smooth first. From a purely practical standpoint, I like my sub girls smooth for precisely that reason — better access. Nothing hidden, no obstructions. By the same token, it's a sensual offering — it indicates a willingness on the part of the sub to hide nothing, to hold nothing back from her Master. Don't you agree?"

"Oh. I, um..." Jaime swallowed, looking sweetly flustered. "Isn't that kind of drastic?"

Donovan shrugged. "Why? Hair grows back. It's just for the weekend. I think it would make your submissive experience more genuine. And then there is the matter of the wax and the whip." He let the sentence hang, again watching the play of emotions on her face, as transparent as if she were speaking aloud.

"Okay," she whispered.

"You're forgetting protocol, sub girl. How do you address your Master?"

Jaime's eyes flashed with a dominant spark, but as he stared her down, she finally amended, "Yes, Sir."

After dinner, he led her into the master bathroom. He got out a big, thick towel and placed it on the linen cabinet in the corner of the room. The cabinet was higher than the counters, the perfect height to provide easy access while he shaved her. He turned on the tap to get the water hot and got a large plastic bowl from beneath the sink. He filled the bowl and added a special scent-free massage oil he'd found worked very well for shaving sensitive skin. He placed the bowl, a pair of barber scissors and a fresh razor on the counter beside the cabinet and turned to Jaime. "Up you go."

Jaime frowned. "Wait. What? I'm going to do it myself. In the shower."

Donovan shook his head. "No, you're not. I'll do it. You just sit back and relax. Leave it all to the Master."

She made no move. Donovan felt a sudden rush of irritated impatience. Was everything a fight with this willful girl? *Patience*, he reminded himself. Jaime still considered herself a dominant with him, even in the face of what she'd experienced so far. Rome wasn't built in a day, and a woman who had identified as a Domme all her adult life wouldn't suddenly become his willing submissive, even if he'd made her fly.

"Jaime," Donovan said in a calm voice, as if coaxing a skittish animal. "Please trust me. I know what I'm doing. I can do it much better than you can do it yourself, bending and reaching in the shower. I'm using a safety razor and I know how to properly prep the skin. You've done beautifully so far today, Jaime. Don't disappoint me now. Show me your courage and your strength of will. Submit with the grace I know you possess."

Slowly she nodded and moved toward the linen cabinet. Donovan helped her up and positioned her so her ass balanced on the edge, her legs spread on either side of her offered cunt as she leaned back against the wall and rested on her elbows.

The desire to drop his jeans and push his cock into her soft heat nearly overwhelmed him, but Donovan kept himself under control and focused on his task. First he clipped away what he could of the auburn pubic curls, dropping the hair into the trashcan. Then he dipped a washcloth into the steaming, oiled water and draped it over her mons.

While it warmed her skin, he reached for her face and leaned down to kiss her. He'd just meant to kiss her lightly, lips closed, but she opened her mouth, her tongue gliding over his lips, which parted of their own accord. They kissed for nearly a minute, and

Donovan had to force himself to pull away before he lost all control.

He took the washcloth from her body and reached for the bottle of massage oil. He squeezed several tablespoons into his hand and then gently stroked it into her skin. Taking the razor, he carefully shaved every bit of hair, moving his fingers along behind the razor until her skin was as smooth as a baby's.

His mouth actually watered as he imagined putting his head down between her spread legs and tasting her silky sweetness. Instead, he helped her down from the cabinet and led her to the full length mirror. "There," he pronounced. "It's done."

Jaime stared at her body, her mouth opening into a small O, though she said nothing.

"It's time for your session," Donovan informed her.

He led her to the playroom. She waited, watching while he placed a plastic sheet beneath the padded spanking horse. He retrieved a red paraffin candle the size of a large aerosol can from the toy cabinet, along with a box of matches. He lit the candle and set it carefully on the small table he kept near the spanking horse.

He had Jaime lie on her back over the horse. He positioned her so her feet were flat on the floor, her newly-smooth cunt fully exposed. He cuffed her wrists together beneath the horse and clipped her ankle cuffs to the legs of the spanking horse. He added leather straps at her calves and thighs, buckling her firmly into place against the legs of the spanking horse so she couldn't move her legs an inch.

He stepped back to admire his handiwork. She looked beautiful tethered to the horse, her arched body accentuating her soft, full breasts tipped with dark pink, fully erect nipples and her smooth cunt, bared to reveal its petal-like folds.

Jaime's eyes were on the candle, in which a small puddle of melted wax had already accumulated. Donovan lifted the candle and moved close to the naked, bound girl.

"You ready?" he asked softly, eager to begin the erotic torture.

"Yes, Sir," she replied, a small tremor moving through her form.

Donovan held the candle high as he let the first drops of bright red liquid drop on Jaime's stomach. She flinched as the hot wax made contact, though Donovan knew it didn't hurt, not from the height at which he'd let it fall. He continued this way for a while, speckling her body with droplets of red. When he felt her relax some, he lowered the candle to increase the heat of the wax when it landed.

He aimed for her left nipple. This drew the first cry of actual pain, the breathy, erotic sound going directly to Donovan's already hard cock. He let a series of drops follow the first, coating her nipple with the red wax. He did the same to the second nipple, as Jaime continued to gasp and jerk in her bonds. When Donovan was satisfied with the coverage, he let the candle glide down her body again, this time hovering over her smooth mons.

The first drop fell on freshly shaven skin. Jaime gasped. Donovan let several more drops fall, lowering the candle each time so she would feel the wax's heat more intensely as it landed. When a drop splashed onto the hood of her clit, Jaime squealed, writhing in a vain effort to move away from the melted wax.

"Stay still," Donovan barked. With his left hand, he spread Jaime's labia wide to expose her cunt completely.

Jaime lifted her head to watch him with wide, frightened eyes. "No," she cried, her voice trembling. "I'm scared. It's going to hurt too much."

"I won't give you more than you can handle, Jaime. You can take a lot more than you think you can. You're my brave girl. Show me how strong you are." He watched her carefully. Her eyes were stark with fear. He waited a beat. If she said her safeword, he would set the candle down. But she said nothing. She nodded slightly and let her head fall back.

Thrilled, Donovan continued. He held the candle high to keep from burning her as he let drop after drop splash down onto the tender folds of her spread cunt. Jaime jerked, shuddered and moaned, but she was handling it beautifully. He didn't stop until her cunt appeared to be covered by a red wax bowl.

Satisfied, Donovan blew out the candle and set it carefully on the table. He moved to the rack and selected a single tail whip. When he returned to her, Jaime lifted her head, her eyes coming into focus as she stared at the whip in his hand.

"Now," he said with a wicked grin. "We whip it off."

~*~

At first Jaime couldn't feel the flick of the whip as its tip made contact with the layer of hardened wax covering her spread pussy. But she could hear it, and the snapping sound made her jump.

Then the wax cracked, bits of it falling away. The whip struck again, this time snapping against the tender skin of her mons. Jaime screamed. The whip moved, its tip flicking painfully over her stomach and breasts. Bits of red wax flew. When the whip curled around her nipple, Jaime screamed again.

She could feel the sweat prickling under her arms and pooling at the small of her back. She couldn't seem to catch her breath, which shuddered from her in gasping pants. Her heart was thudding, skipping a beat with each fiery flick of the whip against her breasts, her nipples, her stomach, her mons. She strained in her bonds and whipped her head from side to the side, the only part of her body she could move.

The thought of her safeword slid into her mind but she shook it away. *I can do this,* she found herself thinking suddenly, furiously. *I can do this!*

But then the whip moved downward, returning to her cunt, flicking away the remaining wax. Jaime's hands were curled into tight fists, her fingernails digging into her palms. Her body was shaking and her heart felt like it was going to explode out of her chest.

"Please," she gasped. "No! Don't do it. Don't hurt me. I can't take it!"

Donovan said only, "Trust me." He continued to flick the bits of wax away from her spread, defenseless cunt. Somehow the Master managed to keep the fiery tip of the whip from making direct contact with her labia, though Jaime remained rigid with fearful anticipation.

The whole experience—being bound in that awkward, exposed position, feeling the sudden, wet singe of melted wax on her skin, and then the stinging kiss of the whip—had left her exhausted and terrified, but at the same time, also thrilled deep in her bones. Her body was thrumming with endorphins, but beyond the "runner's high" of the erotic pain, something else was at play.

Jaime continued to tremble, but at the same time she became aware of the aching throb of lust deep inside her. Was it just system-overload at the hands of a pro? Was it just the fact she was naked and completely exposed to the relentless biting kiss of his whip? Or was it the man himself that pulled this fierce longing from deep within her?

Jaime's mind began to empty as the Master continued to whip every bit of wax from her stinging, tortured skin. All she knew was that she wanted the Master with every fiber of her being. She longed for Donovan to set down his whip and instead drape her body with his. She ached to feel his cock thrusting deep inside her — filling her, claiming her.

As if reading her mind, Donovan at last lay down the whip. He bent over her, unclipping her cuffs and unbuckling the straps around her legs. But instead of stripping and positioning himself between her legs, Donovan put his arms beneath Jaime and lifted her from the spanking horse. He carried her a short distance to a large bondage table, where he lay her gently down.

Beside the table was another candle, this one set into a white square porcelain container about the size of a creamer, one corner shaped like a spout. Donovan lit the wick at its center. Jaime lay still, too spent even to protest, though she did *not* want any more hot wax dripped on her skin, which stung all over from the whip.

"You did great, Jaime," Donovan said, his deep voice a sensual growl. He stroked her cheek, the tips of his fingers rough but welcome on her face, like a kitten's tongue. "With each exercise you show me your true submission. Again and again I see it. Any Master would be proud to call you his sub."

Though Jaime tried to tell herself his claims of her "true submission" were only so much nonsense, she couldn't deny the hot rush of pride his words engendered. Not that she wanted to be anyone's sub.

Did she?

"Don't move," Donovan ordered. "I'll be right back."

He said don't move, but he didn't say don't look, and Jaime followed Donovan with her eyes as he walked to a corner of the large playroom. He opened a mini refrigerator and pulled something out of it. Turning on the tap in the small sink beside the refrigerator, he held whatever was in his hands beneath the running water for a few seconds.

When he returned to Jaime, he showed her what rested on a hand towel. Jaime stared at it, trying to figure out what the heck it was. It looked like a vibrator wrapped in a condom. "This is an ice dildo," Donovan said, lifting the phallus from the towel and holding it up for her anxious inspection. "I love the dichotomy of fire and ice, of heat and cold, of pleasure and pain."

He walked around the bondage table to stand between Jaime's legs. "Feet flat on the table, knees bent," he instructed, lifting her legs to help her into the position he wanted. He reached for a tube of lubricant on the nearby counter and squirted some over the head of the frozen dildo. Stepping between her spread knees, he placed the icy tip of it at her entrance.

Jaime tensed when he began to push the slick, fat ice pop into her. It didn't hurt, but it filled her completely with its icy hardness. "Oooh, that's cold!" Jaime blurted, shuddering. She started instinctively to wrap her arms around her torso, as if that would warm her, but Donovan stopped her.

"Arms at your sides. I'm not going to bind you on the table. You're going to exercise self-control. You will lie still, arms at your sides, legs spread as they are now, feet flat. Make sure you keep that dildo inside of you. Don't you dare push it out, no matter how cold it makes you. Got it?"

"Yes, Sir," Jaime managed, though she shuddered as the frozen phallus chilled her from the inside out.

Donovan reached into the back pocket of his jeans and extracted a black sleep mask. "Once again," he said, as he fitted the mask over her eyes, "I want you to simply accept what I do to you. Don't anticipate.

This blindfold will help in the process. Accept that you are my possession right now. Mine to do with as I will."

Jaime let out a shuddery breath at this pronouncement, though in her bones she knew she was safe with this man. She could hear him moving beside her, and she caught a whiff of caramelized vanilla that she presumed must be the candle wax. The ice was melting inside its latex sheath, but was still a shivery, invading presence inside her.

Jaime felt something splash on her stomach and she squealed with fear, waiting for the burn. But instead of scalding wax, whatever it was on her skin was deliciously warm. Jaime hiccupped in her confusion and relief. She felt Donovan's hand as he massaged what she realized must be oil into her skin.

"You know," he said softly, his voice near her ear, "there's such a focus on the erotic pain and sexual aspects of submission. But there's a bigger picture, at least there should be. To complete the circle of a D/s connection, it's important that the pain and sexual tension be balanced by the sub's knowledge that she is safe and cherished."

Jaime couldn't stop the soft moan of pleasure that escaped her lips as Donovan rubbed the warm, scented oil into her breasts and stomach. Her nipples stiffened to points beneath his palms and she could feel a rush of sexual heat steadily melting the ice dildo inside her.

As Donovan continued to massage and stroke her body, Jaime could feel her heart and breathing slow. Her sexual desire hadn't abated, but only coiled more deeply inside her, glowing hot at the core of her being.

She groaned with unbridled pleasure when the Master's fingers, newly slick with the warm oil, finally grazed her cunt. His fingers stoked her lust back into a blaze, despite the ice still melting inside her. She began to shudder, the rise of an orgasm moving like liquid heat through her body.

Then the hand was withdrawn.

Jaime couldn't stop the sudden cry of dismay. She felt the blindfold being removed and she blinked for a few seconds as her eyes came into focus. Donovan was standing just beside her head, his crotch level with her face. She couldn't help but notice the substantial bulge in his jeans.

"Slide up on the table so your head is hanging off the end," Donovan instructed. Jaime bit back the sigh of sexual frustration as she forced herself to move into the ordered position. What was he planning now?

*Don't anticipate.*

Donovan pulled off his shirt, revealing his muscular chest, the pecs well-defined and covered with dark curling chest hair. While Jaime admired the eye candy of his broad shoulders and sexy chest, Donovan unbuckled his belt and then unbuttoned and unzipped his fly. Jaime watched hungrily as he pulled the jeans, along with his underwear, down his thighs. His cock was as big as the rest of him, the fat head bobbing inches from her face. He moved to stand just behind her head.

"Open your mouth wide. Don't try to do anything except receive me. Keep your throat open. If you can't breathe and it's too much, you can close your hand into a fist and then open it. But only do that if you think you might pass out. Otherwise, accept that I'll keep you safe. I'll pay close attention to your body and your reactions. All you have to do is take what I give you. Can you do that, Jaime?"

"Yes, Sir," Jaime breathed, her eyes fixed on his huge erection. She was good at giving head, and loved doing it. One of the things she loved about it was the absolute control it gave her over a man. But the Master had completely turned the tables on her, taking away every vestige of control by the position he'd placed her in, even down to controlling her very breath with his cock.

She opened her mouth and Donovan moved closer, placing the head of his cock against her tongue. He moved forward slowly, his cock filling her mouth and gliding along her tongue until the head was lodged at the back of her throat. He remained that way for several long seconds, during which Jaime realized she couldn't draw her breath. In the position she was in, his cock was effectively blocking her windpipe. He was, as he'd promised, literally controlling her ability to breathe.

A surge of panic shot through her at a gut level, but she willed herself to remain calm. Time after time Donovan had proved she could trust him. *I'll keep you safe.* He was paying attention. She didn't have to anticipate or worry or think at all. All she had to do was relax and accept what he gave her.

A burning sensation began to mount in her lungs and desperately she willed herself to be calm. A silent scream was building inside her when he finally stepped back and withdrew his cock from her gaping mouth.

Jaime gasped for air, gratefully sucking in the oxygen. Donovan didn't give her much recovery time, however, his cock again sliding back into her mouth. He repeated the exercise over and over, until Jaime's entire focus, her entire world, was his cock filling her mouth and throat.

During one especially long time during which he kept his cock deep in her throat, Jaime felt herself becoming lightheaded. Even so, that initial surge of panic didn't return. She could trust the Master. He would never let harm come to her. She was his vessel, to be used as it pleased him. This realization at once shocked and thrilled her. What was happening to her?

Finally he began to move faster, his rock-hard cock thrusting in and out of her mouth. At the same time she felt his fingers at her cunt, and then ice dildo, now mostly melted, was pulled from her body, leaving her empty and aching to be filled.

"Lift your hips," Donovan ordered in a husky voice. "Keep your leg spread and offer your cunt. Stay in that position, no matter what I do to you."

Eagerly Jaime obeyed, so aroused she knew she would come from just a few strokes. She grunted in startled surprise against the cock filling her mouth when, instead of stroking her, he smacked her cunt hard. Instinctively she lowered her body, her legs slamming shut.

"Back in position!" Donovan barked. "Now!"

Jaime obeyed with a peculiar mix of reluctance and desire, her throbbing cunt still stinging from the blow. He struck her again, but followed up this time with a soothing, sensual stroke of his fingers, which instantly erased the sting. Again and again he alternated between stinging swats and sensual strokes. Jaime shuddered and trembled, struggling to accommodate his girth down her throat while processing the onslaught of pleasure and pain he delivered with his hand.

When he pressed his finger inside her, his palm grinding against her clit, Jaime realized she was coming, and there wasn't a thing she could do to stop it. She couldn't even ask permission, not with the Master's huge cock thrusting in and out of her mouth. She bucked against his hand, mewling ineffectually against the shaft pummeling her mouth and throat. All at once he pulled out, leaving her gasping, tremors of her orgasm still wracking her body.

Leaning over her, he took his cock in his other hand, while still keeping one hand on her spasming cunt. He groaned softly and she felt hot spurts of jism landing against her chest and breasts. Finally he pulled his hand from her cunt. She could smell the redolent scent of her juices and his, and despite the orgasm, her cunt continued to ache with longing.

Donovan stepped away from her, returning with a hand towel, which he used to wipe away his ejaculate from her body. He reached beneath her shoulders.

"Can you sit?"

Jaime nodded and he helped her to a sitting position on the bondage table. From there he helped her off the table, keeping a steadying arm around her shoulders until he saw she could stand on her own.

He moved to stand in front of her, placing his hands on her shoulders. "You doing okay?" he asked, looking into her eyes, his full attention on her.

Jaime nodded, realizing suddenly it was this complete attention to his charge that made him so masterful, as much as his technique and skill. "Yes, Sir," she said, holding back a nearly overwhelming impulse to wrap her arms around him and never, ever let go.

He looked into her eyes a moment longer and then stepped back, apparently satisfied. He grinned suddenly, his eyes sparking with fire. "Time for a hot bath and then bed. You should get some rest. You're going to need it."

# Chapter 10

*Buzz, buzz…buzz buzz…*

Donovan opened his eyes, his sleep-fogged brain trying to process the sound that was interfering with a very erotic dream. A part of his brain switched on, informing him it was his cell phone and he should answer it.

He sat up, reaching for the phone beside his bed, intent on sending the call to voicemail. He glanced down at Jaime, who was curled on her side at the foot of the bed, her cuffed and loosely chained hands tucked beneath the soft curve of her cheek. His cock, in full morning-erection mode, twitched with desire.

*Buzz, buzz…buzz buzz…*

Donovan focused on the phone screen, his finger poised over the *decline call* feature. Then he saw who it was. *Shit.*

Sliding out of bed, he grabbed the pair of boxer shorts he'd left on the floor by the bed and padded quickly to the bathroom as he took the call. He wasn't scheduled for a shift today, was he?

"Gordon? What's up?"

"Dude. Sorry to bother you so early but it's kind of an emergency." If Donovan hadn't seen Gordon's name on the screen, he wouldn't have recognized his voice.

"Whoa. You sound like shit. Flu?"

"I think so, yeah," Gordon rasped. "I'm running a temperature. My bones ache."

"Sucks. What can I do for you?" Donovan asked with a sinking feeling.

"It's the Filmore Street Fair. I signed up for the vaccination tent but no way can I do it like this, obviously. Of course Mike will be there to run the thing, but with the crowds we've been having, he definitely needs a second volunteer. I tried Bernard and Mandy already, but neither one can get away this morning. If there was any way you could take my shift—" Gordon interrupted himself with a long, phlegmy coughing fit.

Donovan glanced out the bathroom door at the sleeping beauty for whom he had lots of delicious, devious plans for the day. His brain was already forming his excuses when Gordon added, "Several of the homeless shelters in the area are working with us to get folks at risk for Hepatitis B vaccinated. There were lines around the block yesterday. The response has been huge." When Donovan still didn't answer, Gordon added, "It's just for three hours, from ten to one. Can you cover for me?"

Donovan glanced at the wall clock—7:45. He sighed inwardly, his sense of duty superseding his intense desire to continue with Jaime where they'd left off the night before. "Okay, sure. I can do it. Give me the details."

When he returned to the bedroom Donovan saw Jaime was awake. She was lying on her back, her cuffed wrists on her chest between her bare breasts, the sheet covering her lower half. A dozen hot scenarios flashed through his mind, but they would have to wait. Still, he could at least start the morning by making sure his temporary sub girl remained in the proper mindset, however fleeting any morning session would be.

"Good morning, Jaime. Did you sleep well?"

"I guess so, Sir." She held up her cuffed wrists. "I mean, as well as can be expected. I've never slept in chains before."

"You'll get used to it," Donovan replied with a grin. "Do you need to use the toilet?"

Jaime nodded. "Yes, Sir."

"Come on, then."

Jaime slid out of bed, her movements made somewhat awkward by her cuffed wrists and ankles. He'd chained both sets of cuffs before directing her to climb into bed the night before, leaving plenty of play in the chains. They were intended to be more of a symbolic reminder of her status than an actual restraint.

He'd had to exercise his own restraint with a vengeance, overruling his powerful desire to pull the naked girl at his feet up into his arms. He knew if he'd done that, however, he would not have been able to control his need to fuck her. Which he would do before their time together was up. But not yet. Not yet.

His cock hardened as he watched her hobble forward in her chains, making her way toward him. When she stood before him, a lock of red hair falling into her eyes, Donovan instructed, "Hold up your wrists." He released the chains and removed the cuffs.

Jaime gripped her wrists, her fingers stroking the area that had been covered with leather since she'd arrived the day before. Crouching, Donovan released the ankle cuffs as well, leaving the restraints on the bureau before leading Jaime into the bathroom.

He watched as she sat on the toilet. As before, she kept her face averted while she peed. Suddenly she looked up with a grimace. "Donovan, uh, Sir," she said, her tone urgent. "I have to—can you leave me alone? Please, I really need to…" She trailed off, the sentence incomplete though her meaning was clear.

Donovan shook his head, amused. "After what you've experienced so far with me, do you really think there's anything left to hide, Jaime? A sub keeps nothing from her Master. Nothing. Modesty is not an option in a fully-realized D/s relationship."

Jaime groaned softly, a mutinous expression moving over her very expressive face. Donovan decided to cut her a little slack since she wasn't, after all, *his* sub girl. He didn't leave the bathroom, but he did turn away, heading toward the sink. He turned on the water and busied himself brushing his teeth, sneaking surreptitious glances in the mirror at the girl as she emptied her bowels, her face flaming red.

When she'd flushed the toilet, Donovan turned on the shower. "I put your shampoo and conditioner in there. Don't worry about grooming. I'll take care of that for you later. Right now just wash up quickly, and then present yourself for inspection in the bedroom. I'll be waiting."

While Jaime showered, Donovan went to the kitchen and put on a pot of coffee. He couldn't decide if he should leave her at home or take her with him. He could, he realized, explain the situation and send her on her way. After all, his point had certainly been made—despite her dominant persona, at her core Jaime was deeply submissive, at least with him. Even as the thought of letting her go early occurred to him, he dismissed it out of hand. The bet had been for forty-eight hours—it wouldn't be fair to either of them to cut it short.

He knew he was lying to himself. It wasn't really about fair, was it?

It was about desire.

Donovan pushed this thought aside. If she had hired him to train her, rather than just fulfilling the terms of their bet, he wouldn't have given his decision two thoughts. He would have left her at home, properly naked, with specific tasks to complete during his absence. But she hadn't hired him, and she wasn't a sub in training.

She was — what was she?

A beautiful young woman who had responded to each new experience with passion and honesty. A strong, sassy spitfire of a girl who had previously defined herself as purely dominant, but appeared to have the courage to embrace the submissive part of herself he was helping her to uncover and explore. The bottom line, he realized, was that he didn't want to be apart from her, even for four hours.

He returned to the bedroom, coffee mug in hand. Jaime was toweling her hair in the bathroom. She caught his eye in the mirror as he sat on the bed. She hung the towel on a rack and came out of the bathroom, her hair damp and sweetly tousled, her skin rosy. She stopped in front of him, crossing her arms uncertainly.

"Hands behind your neck, back arched, feet shoulder-width apart," Donovan instructed. He stood, setting the mug on the night table, and approached the naked young woman. Her breasts were thrust out provocatively by her position, and he resisted an impulse to dip his head and take a nipple into his mouth.

Instead he put his hand on her throat, his fingers pressing lightly on either side of her jaw. He watched her face as he applied gentle but steady pressure. She reacted as she had the first time he'd done this—her eyes widening, the pupils dilating, her lips parting, her breath quickening. Clearly this was a trigger for her—the hand on the throat did more than a thousand words could do to place her quickly into a submissive headspace.

When he released her throat, she sighed, leaning slightly forward, her body language as clear as any spoken word. *Don't stop.* Interesting. He would love to explore breath play with her, but not now. There was no time this morning.

Instead he moved his hands along her arms, stroking her armpits with his fingers and then drawing his hands down her sides and back up to her breasts. While staring into her eyes, he found her nipples, feeling them stiffen and swell as he rolled them between his forefingers and thumbs. Her lips parted again, a small cry of pain escaping when he twisted the engorged nipples. He twisted harder, his cock springing to aching attention. After a minute, he let her go and stepped back.

He went to the bureau and retrieved a small flashlight. "Bend over and grip your ankles. Keep your legs spread. I'm going to inspect your cunt and asshole."

Jaime stared at the flashlight, color moving once again over her cheeks. Donovan silently dared her to disobey, holding her gaze in his. Finally she lowered her arms and bent forward, reaching for her ankles. She was limber, her legs straight as she held her position. Donovan moved around behind her and crouched, flicking on the flashlight and moving it over her ass and sex from behind.

She had a perfect pink pucker between her ass cheeks, and a gorgeous, pouty cunt. Of course, he already knew that. The point of this procedure was more about erotic humiliation and control. That Jaime was willing to subject herself to the exercise was further proof in Donovan's mind of the submissive fire burning deep inside her.

He could fuck her now, right here. He could grab her hips and thrust into her from behind, not even taking the time to lead her to the bed, instead just pushing her to the carpet as he sank his rock-hard cock into her wet heat.

Donovan shook his head to break the sexual spell that was weaving around him. Plans had changed. He was a grownup who could control his impulses. And he'd promised Gordon he'd step in. He needed to let Jaime know what was going on.

"Okay. You may stand up," he said, annoyed that his voice came out hoarse with lingering lust. He cleared his throat, adding. "Let's go have some breakfast. I need to talk to you about something."

Once they were at the table, Jaime in her place on the cushion at his feet, Donovan fed her and himself scrambled eggs and bacon, along with coffee and orange juice. It felt so right, somehow, to have this woman kneeling beside him. As if she'd always been there.

Donovan realized he knew next to nothing about Jaime, nor she about him, and yet the connection between them had been instant and strong. He found himself looking forward to getting to know more about her, both in and out of the scene.

As they ate, Donovan could see the question in Jaime's eyes about what he wanted to talk about, but he was pleased to note she didn't speak since she hadn't been asked a direct question. Finally, Donovan set down the fork. "Something came up this morning. I'm going to have to step in for a fellow medic who's sick. There's a street fair later this morning, and our volunteer firehouse has a tent to give vaccinations to the homeless."

Jaime raised her eyebrows. "You're a medic? I'm confused."

Donovan nodded. "Yeah. I run the club with Gene now, but before that I was a fulltime paramedic with an ambulance corps. I still do volunteer work to keep my skills up, and also because it's the right thing to do. I can't take the night shifts anymore, obviously, but I work a couple of mornings a week, sometimes riding the ambulance to 911 calls, but mostly doing stuff like working at these street fairs and free clinics. A guy I work with is out sick. He called this morning, begging me to cover for him."

"Oh." The single word was laden with disappointment. Jaime's crestfallen expression tugged at Donovan's heart. He realized he hadn't made himself clear.

"I'm not suggesting we cut your training short. Not at all. I was thinking, if you wanted to, you could come with me to the fair. Of course, I would expect you to remain in proper sub mode, and as such I would provide certain, uh, incentives, to make sure you did so."

Jaime flashed such a dazzling smile at Donovan that he laughed with delight. "I take it that's a yes?"

"Yes. Yes, Sir."

~*~

Jaime shifted on the folding chair, trying to adjust to the fullness of the butt plug and flexible dildo Donovan had inserted before they left his house. In addition to the phalluses filling her ass and cunt, beneath her long, flowing skirt she was wearing special panties that contained a fitted butterfly vibrator Donovan had tucked against her clit. The wireless remote was in his shirt pocket.

She watched Donovan and the other man who had been introduced to her as Mike as they sat at either end of a long table with their disposable syringes, cotton balls and alcohol, expertly inoculating the long line of mostly women and children waiting patiently for their turn.

When they'd arrived at the open-air tent, Donovan had Jaime sit near the edge of the tent wall to his left, partially hidden in shadow. It felt strange to be just sitting there instead of helping out, but she reasoned she would probably get in their way. Mike and Donovan seemed to have everything well under control.

As she watched Donovan at work, she realized she'd never really imagined him as anything but the Master, always in Dom mode, 24/7. Seeing him in this new light gave him an added dimension in her mind. She found that she quite liked this new side of him—the altruistic volunteer, giving of his time and expertise because it was "the right thing to do."

The sudden whirring at Jaime's clit startled her out of her reverie. She glanced sharply at Donovan, recalling his words earlier that morning. "Two important aspects of submission," Donovan had lectured as he had eased the phalluses into her body, "are discipline and self-control. While I'm doing my work this morning, you will sit quietly, hands folded in your lap. You aren't yet properly trained to override your physical impulses, and I get that. Nevertheless, no matter how much you want to come, you will resist as long as you possibly can. When you do come, you'd better do it as discreetly as you can, again for obvious reasons. There will be a cost, however. I want you to keep track of how many times you climax. You will be punished for each orgasm when we return to the house."

Jaime hadn't tried to protest this inherently unfair edict. After all, she'd played the same game with her sub boys, teasing them to ejaculation, and then punishing them for coming. Today's promised punishment, she realized with a frightened thrill, was probably going to be a lot more intense than the slap and tickle games she'd played back at Betsy's club, in what already seemed like a different lifetime.

Donovan's hand moved casually to his shirt pocket, a small smile lifting his lips. He didn't turn to look directly at Jaime, but she was fairly certain he could see her in his peripheral vision. Jaime shifted on the chair, crossing and uncrossing her legs in an effort to ease the constant, stimulating tickle at her clit.

She hadn't even been with Donovan a full twenty-four hours, and already she felt as if she never wanted to leave him. Each new experience, since the moment she'd arrived the afternoon before, had been more intense and mind blowing than the last. Her entire notion of herself as a dominant had been completely shaken, like a kaleidoscope being tipped and turned, the pieces of her psyche aligning and realigning into patterns she never would have believed possible. Yet somehow, with each startling revelation, the Master had kept her feeling safe, and not only that, but longing for more.

Jaime realized her mouth had fallen open, her breathing coming in rapid, shallow pants. She shifted again on the chair, closing her mouth and pressing her thighs together. She watched a child of about three who sat in his mother's arms, squirming and crying as Donovan quickly inoculated the boy. "All done, big guy!" Donovan produced a red lollypop from a bowl, holding it out to the boy, whose crying promptly stopped as he reached for the candy.

The steady whirring continued at Jaime's cunt and she shuddered. Donovan turned suddenly, looking at her head on. He smiled, laugh lines radiating from his brilliantly blue eyes as he reached once more into his shirt pocket. The whirring suddenly intensified, making Jaime gasp involuntarily. Again she pressed her lips together, breathing hard through her nose.

She glanced at Mike at the far end of the table, relieved that he wasn't paying her the slightest bit of attention, still busy with his own line of patients. She looked back at the Master, who had continued to watch her while a large man settled himself precariously on the small folding chair facing Donovan and rolled up his sleeve. All at once, before she could even entirely process what was happening to her, a rush of overwhelming sensation surged through her groin and she began to tremble, tumbling into an orgasm right there in front of everyone.

Only Donovan, thank god, seemed to realize what was happening to her. He cocked his head, his eyes blazing into her as she shuddered in her attempts to remain still and quiet while the orgasm washed over her. Finally Donovan turned back to the man waiting for his shot, reaching into his shirt pocket as he did so. Mercifully, this time he turned the remote down to a steady but tolerable hum, though even that small amount of stimulation was hard to bear in her hyper-aroused state.

Donovan continued to adjust the remote as the hours passed, sometimes turning it so high Jaime was afraid everyone around them would hear the whirring between her legs, though to her great relief, no one seemed to notice above the hubbub of the fair. Sometimes he turned it off completely for a while, only to restart it when Jaime had drifted into a nearly-dozing state in her chair.

The whole experience was a major exercise in patience and self-control, as he'd warned her it would be. Left to her own devices, Jaime wasn't the type of person to sit still doing nothing for five minutes, much less three hours. Being forced to do so was curiously freeing, and she found herself relaxing in a way that was unfamiliar but somehow welcome.

This didn't happen right away, however. For the first hour, in between bouts of erotic torture with the butterfly, Jaime found herself constantly shifting and fidgeting, her fingers tapping on her thighs, her legs bouncing. But as the time passed, she found herself settling into a kind of peaceful stillness. She didn't have to do anything except sit there quietly, waiting for the Master to finish his work. True, there was the challenge of resisting and then controlling the orgasms that threatened to overwhelm her from time to time, but even that exercise took on a kind of restful life of its own after a while — a rhythm of arousal, control, surrender and recovery.

When the tent was finally closed for a lunch break, Donovan stood from his seat and stretched his arms over his head, causing the trio of snakes on his left biceps to undulate. He shook hands with Mike, who thanked him for standing in for Gordon, and then turned to Jaime, holding out his hand. "Ready to go?"

Jaime took his hand, allowing him to pull her up. He kept her hand in his as he led her through the throng of people crowding the street. She walked a little awkwardly toward his car, the phalluses still buried inside her. She was exhausted, she realized, her legs wobbling slightly. All those orgasms could take it out of a girl.

Once they were in the car, Donovan turned to her. "How many times?"

Jaime blew out a breath, her stomach suddenly clenching with anxious anticipation. "Eight. I think," she replied honestly.

Donovan lifted his eyebrows. "You think?"

Jaime looked away from his penetrating gaze. "Yeah. I mean, yes, Sir. Sometimes I wasn't sure where one started and the other left off. It was, um, pretty intense sometimes."

To her relief, Donovan just laughed. "Was it, now?" He began to drive, weaving through the traffic down a long, steep hill. "Eight times, huh," he mused quietly, grinning to himself, his eyes on the road. "Someone's due for some serious punishment."

# Chapter 11

It felt strange to be sitting across from Donovan in the little café they'd decided to stop at for lunch after leaving the fair. In just the short time she'd spent at his house, she'd already gotten used to, indeed, found she quite liked, kneeling naked on a cushion at his feet while he fed her with such loving attention. The experience was not only an exercise in submission. It was also highly erotic and at the same time, oddly comforting.

She was very aware of the black leather tote bag that rested on the empty chair beside her. Inside were the phalluses and the butterfly panties she'd worn in the tent. Donovan had handed her the bag when they entered the café, instructing her to go to the bathroom and remove the items before joining him at the table.

Menus and glasses of water had appeared while she was in the bathroom, and a waitress came by now to take their orders. They decided to share a pizza. While they were waiting for the food, the waitress returned with a carafe of red wine and two wineglasses.

"I hope you don't mind," Donovan said with a smile. "I took the liberty of ordering while you were in the bathroom." They watched as the waitress filled their glasses and then left with the promise to return soon with the pizza.

Donovan picked up his glass and held it aloft. "A toast. To taking risks and discovering new things."

Jaime clinked her glass lightly against his, a smile her only response.

"This is just a break, you know. Your forty-eight hours aren't over yet."

Jaime swallowed, nodding, as her heart did a little somersault in her chest. She didn't want it to be over. Not now. Not yet.

Donovan took another drink of wine and set down his glass. "So tell me about yourself, Jaime. Gene mentioned something about your leaving New York rather abruptly. What brought you to San Francisco?"

"Truth?" Jaime said, taking another large sip of her wine.

"Naturally," Donovan replied.

"The west coast was as far as I could get from New York."

"A guy?" Donovan asked softly, his expression suddenly hard to read.

Jaime shook her head. "No. I guess it was just system overload. It had gotten to the point where I dreaded even getting out of bed each morning. My job sucked, my boss sucked, the apartment building I lived in was changing to co-op and I had to either buy in or get out. I wasn't even having fun anymore at the BDSM club where I liked to hang out. Everything had become a drag, all the pleasure drained out of it. I looked around one night and realized I was a gerbil caught running in a wheel, spinning and spinning, but going nowhere."

"So you, what, just got in your car and drove as far away as you could?" Donovan looked both incredulous and amused.

Jaime nodded. "That's about the size of it. Yeah." She shook her head, marveling at her own insanity. "Crazy, right?"

"I think it's great!" Donovan said, his smile lighting his blue eyes. "Very courageous. Which is in keeping with everything I've learned about you this weekend."

Jaime pondered this, feeling ridiculously pleased. "Really? You think I'm courageous?"

Donovan's smile fell away and he nodded soberly. "I do. In spite of misgivings, you found the courage to trust me, but more importantly, yourself. I gave you a lot to handle, Jaime. You didn't white knuckle your way through it either. You were scared some of the time, sure, but you tapped into the power of your submissive nature, and you exhibited extraordinary grace. Any Master would be proud to claim you as his sub."

Jaime held her breath. Was he going to ask her to become his fulltime sub girl? Was she ready to take such a leap after just a weekend together? After all, she was still dominant, at least with every guy except the Master. Did he expect her to throw all that aside? Would she be able to, even if she wanted to?

"So, you ready to pick up the whip again tomorrow, Mistress?" the Master said, as if they were just two colleagues sharing a casual lunch. "You're still going to need to juggle waitressing duties until we can get a replacement. Gene's working on that. We agreed that once word gets out that we have a Mistress in residence, the waiting list for your services will be a mile long."

Jaime felt at once relieved and chagrined that she'd so misjudged what Donovan had been about to say. She answered in a light tone, hoping her laugh didn't sound too forced. "I'll be ready, don't worry. I was born ready."

Donovan laughed in apparent approval. "I believe that. Yes, I do."

The waitress, as if on cue, appeared with their pie and they each took a slice. Jaime welcomed the distraction, as it gave her time to compose herself. They ate the meal in relative silence.

Jaime accepted the offer of a second glass of wine, letting its pleasant buzz relax her. Their time together so far had to be the most bizarre and also the most intensely erotic experience of her life. They had clearly gone far beyond just fulfilling the terms of some bet. Their connection had been deep and immediate. No way Donovan didn't feel it too.

Maybe he was just being sensibly cautious. Surely it was impossible to sustain the stunning level of intensity that existed between them since the minute she'd arrived at his house. Maybe he, too, was feeling his way in whatever it was that was developing between them. Maybe he was just giving her some space, in anticipation of her leaving the next day. Yes, that had to be it. She wouldn't blow it by pushing too hard, too fast. She would go with the flow.

*Stop anticipating. You need to let go. Of everything.*

*Yes, Sir*, Jaime said silently. *Yes, Master Donovan.*

~*~

"As I'm sure you know well from your own experience as a Domme," Donovan said as he stroked the silky soft folds of Jaime's cunt, "a sub must learn to control his or, in this case, her, orgasm, denying herself until it pleases her Master to let her come. By the same token, when he gives her a command to come, she must do so at once." He was kneeling beside the lovely, naked girl, savoring the sweet tremble of her limbs as he teased her with his fingers.

Jaime was draped on her back over a long, low padded adjustable bench, the front legs set lower than the back so that her pelvis was offered up, legs spread wide on either side of the bench. Though she nodded in agreement, something in her face gave Donovan pause.

"What?" he asked. "What are you thinking?" He pushed a finger into her wetness as he asked the question and Jaime let out a small groan, a tremor moving through her body.

"Focus," Donovan admonished, crooking his finger inside her and stroking the soft wetness enveloping it. "Answer the question."

Jaime blew out several breaths through pursed lips as she struggled for control. Finally she managed in a breathy voice, "I get what you're saying in theory. I've never actually had a full time sub or anything close to that, but I did engage in a little orgasm control play back at the club with some guys. Not that they ever managed to control themselves very well." She gave a small laugh, which edged into a moan as Donovan continued to stroke her.

"Go on," he urged. "Finish your thought."

"Oooo," Jaime sighed as Donovan ran his thumb in a light circle over her hard clit. She rallied herself enough to continue, "I understand resisting your orgasm, up to a point, but I don't really get how you can just make yourself come whenever you want, just because your Master says so. I mean, it's a physiological thing, isn't it? I can't just *will* myself to orgasm."

"It's a good question. The answer is that a good Master won't set you up with impossible odds, unless for some reason he wishes you to fail, which is a different scenario than what I'm talking about. When I, I mean your Master, tells you to hold back, it's because he knows you're being stimulated to the point of orgasm, and he wants to measure your ability to control your body to suit his pleasure. So, when he tells you to come, your only job at that point is to *let go*. It's like opening a flood gate. You learn to keep it closed until directed to open it. It's really very simple."

He continued to stroke her, adding a second finger to the first inside the velvet clutch of her hot, wet cunt. Jaime's eyes closed as she groaned, her hips arching upward. He could feel her clit beneath his palm, hard as a little diamond.

"Control yourself," Donovan said sternly. "Stop focusing on your own sexual pleasure. Open your eyes and look at me."

Jaime's eyelids fluttered open and she looked in the direction of his face, though she didn't appear to be focusing. Donovan pulled his fingers, sticky with her juices, away from her yielding body and reached for the riding crop.

"Today you had eight orgasms. I warned you beforehand you would be punished for each orgasm. It seems fitting the focus of the punishment should be your cunt, don't you agree?"

Donovan waited. When Jaime didn't respond, he picked up the riding crop he'd selected for her punishment and smacked her inner thigh sharply with the small rectangular flap of leather.

"Ow!" Jaime cried, slamming her legs together.

"Open your legs!" Donovan ordered. With obvious reluctance, Jaime obeyed. Clearly, she needed a lot more than forty-eight hours to be properly trained. "Now answer the question. Does your cunt deserve to be punished for all those orgasms?"

"Yes, Sir," Jaime finally muttered, though Donovan could tell she wasn't convinced, but only saying what she thought he wanted to hear.

He reminded himself she was new to this side of the D/s equation, and said in a gentler tone, "I know you feel like it's a setup. I put you in a situation where you can't help but come, and then punish you for doing just that. The real point of the exercise is that the Master dictates what happens, and you accept it. You submit, not necessarily because something makes sense to you or works for you, but entirely and only because it pleases your Master. By mutual consent you are his to do with as he pleases. Of course, in a relationship of this kind, the Master has a huge responsibility to keep his sub safe, and if he's worth his salt, he will also cherish and adore her. But the bottom line is, his word is law. You aren't to question his dictates. You just have to obey to the best of your ability and to submit with as much grace as you possess."

He watched as Jaime seemed to absorb this. "I believe your cunt needs to be punished for all those orgasms. Do you agree with that, sub girl?"

"Yes, Sir."

Donovan smiled. "Good girl." He picked up the riding crop. "Tilt your hips so I have full access to your cunt. I'm going to crop you. We'll start slow so you can adjust, but then you'll take eight hard blows directly on your cunt, one for each orgasm. Got it?"

"Yes, Sir," Jaime whispered, her eyes wide.

"And why will you endure this punishment?"

"Because it pleases you, Sir."

Donovan smiled. "Now you're getting it. And to make sure you're a willing participant in the punishment, I want you to hold your cunt open for me. Spread it wide with your fingers. If you let go at any point, we'll have to start over."

Donovan lifted his wet finger to his lips, tasting Jaime's nectar as he studied her reaction. The flash of fear in her eyes, along with the flush rising up her neck and over her cheeks, and the perk of her fully erect nipples told Donovan in no uncertain terms he had Jaime just where he wanted her — balanced on the edge of lust, erotic fear and, yes, longing for what he offered.

She titled her hips provocatively upward and reached for her cunt to spread it wide for her punishment. Donovan moved directly between Jaime's spread legs, shifting back on his knees until he was at the best angle to crop her pretty pussy.

He began lightly, not much more than a firm stroke of black leather against the dark pink labia, which were glistening and swollen with arousal. Almost at once Jaime began to moan, small mewling sounds. Donovan gave her some time to adjust and then, without warning, he let the first real blow land with a thwack.

"One," he intoned over Jaime's squeal. Because she wasn't expecting it, and because she was undisciplined, Jaime let go of her pussy lips as she cried out.

"Back in position," Donovan said calmly, waiting until she obeyed. "And we start over." He struck her again, as hard as before. "One."

She managed to keep her position. "Good girl," Donovan said softly and then, "Two," as he smacked the tender folds. Again Jaime cried out, but she held her position. "Three. Four. Five"

Jaime began to whimper. Her entire body was shaking. Donovan paused, giving her a moment to collect herself, while at the same time heightening the anticipation for the next blow.

Just as an experiment, he asked, "Who do you belong to?"

"You, Sir," Jaime moaned without any hesitation. Something clutched at Donovan's heart, throwing him temporarily off balance. To regain his equilibrium, he smacked at Jaime's exposed inner thighs in a steady series of stinging blows. Her pale skin reddened quickly beneath the leather. Donovan was pleased to see she kept her fingers at her cunt, spreading her labia wide.

Unable to resist a moment longer, Donovan again smacked her exposed, tender folds. "Six."

Jaime yelped and nearly fell out of position, but recalled herself in time. She was panting, tears leaking from the corners of her closed eyes.

"Seven."

Her moan was low and feral, her entire body tensed. Donovan waited, his cock pulsing in his jeans, his balls aching. He wasn't going to be able to hold out much longer. His blood was hot, fired up by her erotic suffering and his fierce desire to claim her.

Leaning forward, he blew lightly on Jaime's wet, swollen cunt. She gasped, her eyes flying open. "That's right." Donovan nodded, holding her gaze captive in his. "Keep your eyes open for the last one."

She began to tremble again, her green eyes swimming with tears that couldn't hide the answering spark of fire that emanated from somewhere deep inside her. He raised the crop over her sex, pulling an anticipatory whimper from the sub girl.

Their mutual desire, heightened by Jaime's erotic fear and the rush of his own sadistic power, moved like an electric current between them. His gaze interlocked with hers, Donovan brought the crop down with a resounding smack.

"Eight."

Jaime cried out, her legs slamming closed as she rolled from the low bench to the floor. Donovan didn't stop her or admonish her for failing to remain in position until released. She was at the very limit of what she could handle, and he knew she'd given him everything she had.

Donovan moved so he was kneeling beside her. He placed a hand lightly on her back as she rocked herself back and forth like a child. He stroked her back and shoulders until her trembling subsided and he felt her body relax.

He stood, reaching down to lift her into his arms. She hid her face, still wet with tears, against his chest as he carried her to the bedroom. Again he felt that unfamiliar clutching at his heart, as if someone, as if Jaime, were reaching into his chest and squeezing.

He laid her gently on the bed and lay down beside her, pulling her into his arms. He was still fully dressed, wearing a T-shirt and jeans, aware if he got naked, he would lose the last toehold of self-control he possessed. Jaime needed some recovery time, and Donovan forced himself to be content with just holding her in his arms.

They lay quietly for several minutes. Donovan felt Jaime's body relax against him, her breath slowing and deepening. He held her tighter, nuzzling his head against the back of her neck, memorizing the feel of her, the smell of her.

What would happen tomorrow?

*Stay in the moment*, Donovan reminded himself. He let his mind empty, slowing his breathing to match that of the sleeping girl beside him. It wasn't long before he felt the tug of sleep pulling him down into the mattress. Giving in, he closed his eyes.

~*~

Later that evening, after a long, hot shower and a simple meal, Donovan led Jaime back into the bedroom. As they stood beside the bed, he lifted her face in his hands. She closed her eyes, her lips parting for a kiss. Donovan's lips met hers, his tongue entering her mouth as he moved one hand across her slender throat.

She gasped lightly against his mouth as he placed his finger and thumb strategically beneath her jaw on either side. With his other hand, he pulled her close. He could feel the erect points of her breasts as he crushed her to his chest, his mouth still locked on hers.

When he let her go, she stumbled back, her mouth still parted like a little bird's, her eyes shining with desire that mirrored his own. Donovan surrendered to temptation, dipping his head to catch one hard nipple in his teeth. He tugged gently and then a little harder, waiting for her small, erotic gasp of pain before closing his lips over the nubbin and swirling his tongue in a circle around it.

Her moan set a jolt of pure fire through his body. He lifted his face to study hers and stroked her cheek. Her skin was fever-hot, her eyes glittering. Unable to hold himself back for another second, Donovan pushed at Jaime's shoulders, forcing her down onto the bed.

"Don't move," he ordered as he reached for his belt, opened his pants and pulled off his shirt, throwing the lot in a heap on the floor. He grabbed the condom packet he'd set on the night table before dinner and tore it open.

Jaime, who was watching him with hungry eyes, shook her head. "I'm protected," she whispered.

With a nod, Donovan dropped the condom, forgetting it as he lifted himself over the beautiful girl with a barely suppressed groan. He'd been waiting all weekend for this, and it had been harder with each passing hour to resist. Only the knowledge that it would diminish Jaime's submissive experience if he gave in too soon had kept his lust at bay.

He kissed her again, his cock like a throbbing bar of steel against her thigh. He lifted his head long enough to murmur urgently, "I want you, Jaime. I *must* have you." Then he kissed her again, loving the taste of her, thrilling to her soft, feminine body. She wrapped her arms around his neck, her pelvis tilting and legs parting beneath him in silent but clear invitation.

He'd planned to draw out the time until he actually penetrated her, teasing her until she begged for it, but now he found he couldn't resist her for even one more second. The entire weekend had been extended foreplay, in a way, all leading toward this moment.

Donovan reached for his cock, guiding the head to her opening. He nudged just the crown inside her slick heat, somehow finding the strength to hold out just a little longer. "You want it?" he teased. "You want your Master to fuck you, slave girl?"

"Yes," Jaime hissed, the *s* sibilant with need. "Please." She arched her body upward.

With a small, sadistic laugh, Donovan held himself back, his cock made even harder by her wanton effort to draw him deeper inside. "Do you deserve to be fucked, Jaime? Have you earned it?"

Even in the throes of her lust, the adorable girl blushed. "Yes, Sir," she whispered, ducking her head downward.

Donovan had never known someone whose emotions were so readily apparent in the flushing of their skin. He felt at once tender and desperate to have her at last. His need was almost painful. "God, I want you so fucking much," he whispered.

He pushed gently into her, moving slowly, giving her time to accommodate his girth. Her cunt was like a wet, silky sheath, the muscles pulling him deeper inside as they clamped around him. Donovan groaned. He wasn't going to be able to last very long, not this first time, anyway. She was just too perfect beneath him, too hot, too sexy, too right.

Donovan's body took over, his entire being exploding in pure, raw pleasure as he thrust deep inside Jaime. He didn't want to come, not yet, so he forced himself to ease up. Reaching up, he pulled Jaime's arms from around his neck and extended them over her head against the bed, letting his weight rest on her wrists as he held her down.

Jaime gasped, her cunt tightening around his shaft. "Ooooo," she moaned, lifting her body as much as she could beneath him. Donovan began to thrust again, no longer able to hold back, not even a little. Jaime began to tremble, making little gasping cries.

Suddenly she stiffened and he could actually feel the spasm of a climax emanating from deep inside her.

That did it—he couldn't hold on anymore, not for another second. He let himself go, still gripping her wrists high over her head as he spurt his seed deep inside her. He felt as if he were melting into the fabric of the universe. He couldn't see, he couldn't hear, he could barely move. His head was spinning, the room humming, the world out of focus.

He must have lost consciousness for a second or two, because when he came to himself he was lying heavily on Jaime, his heart pounding against hers. Their bodies were slick with sweat and his hands were still on her wrists, though he was no longer gripping them.

With an effort, Donovan forced himself up and rolled from her. He lifted himself onto one elbow and stared down at the lovely girl beside him. Jaime lay still, her eyes closed, legs akimbo, arms still extended over her head. Her chest and cheeks were flushed a rosy, orgasmic pink and there was a small, beatific smile on her face. With a happy sigh, Donovan fell back beside her and let his eyes close.

# Chapter 12

"Looks like you have a text message." Donovan held out Jaime's cell phone. It was Tuesday morning and the forty-eight hours were nearing their end. Jaime's phone had sat by the bed untouched during that time. Now the little whistle that indicated a text had caught Donovan's attention.

Jaime, wet hair curling behind her ears, her naked body damp and rosy-hued, took her cell phone. As she looked down at the screen, Donovan admired the lovely young woman. He had definitely approved of Jaime's way of waking him up—her mouth closing warm and wet over his cock and not letting go until he'd pushed her away in his desperation to sink his shaft deep into the wet, perfect curve of her cunt.

He would have asked Gordon to take his shift at the free clinic that afternoon so they could have spent the rest of day making love, but he knew even if Gordon felt one-hundred percent better, he wouldn't have been fever-free long enough to be around the patients.

Donovan told himself it was for the best. Jaime and he had been moving awfully fast, even given the forty-eight hour "anything goes" nature of their weekend. He wouldn't want to give her the wrong impression, after all.

"It's Gene!" Jaime said excitedly. "He found a replacement already. Someone he knows with experience. I don't have to be a waitress anymore, except on an as-needed basis. I get to be a full time Mistress at the club starting tonight!"

Donovan couldn't help but smile at Jaime's eager excitement. "I don't have to be at the free clinic until noon. Your news definitely calls for a celebration. How about I take you to Eve's S&M Toy Box after breakfast? They have great stuff there, top quality. We get a lot of our gear and equipment for the club there. How about a new outfit for Mistress Jaime's debut as Dominatrix in residence? Sound good?"

"Sounds great," Jaime replied with a broad smile. "I've heard about that place. I've been meaning to check it out."

Donovan fed Jaime one last time, thinking how right it felt to have the sub girl kneeling naked at his feet, her small, pretty mouth open to receive sustenance, her big green eyes so sweetly focused on his face as if nothing else existed, nothing else mattered. It was almost as if she, and she alone, belonged there.

Donovan gave himself a mental shake of the shoulders. What was he thinking? He reminded himself of the mantra by which he lived and which had always served him well—*stay in the moment.*

As Donovan weaved his way through the traffic, they traded stories about BDSM scenes that had gone awry over the years in one way or another, laughing at each other's tales of humorous woe. When Jaime reached for Donovan's hand at a traffic light, he intertwined his fingers with hers, their hands fitting perfectly together. He felt as if they'd known each other for years, and it felt good.

He found a parking place reasonably close to the store. Once inside, he grinned as he watched Jaime take in the large space, which was actually a converted warehouse. The place was filled with every kind of BDSM gear and clothing one could imagine, and plenty more one had never even thought of. Even though it was a Tuesday morning, there were plenty of folk milling around, most of them dressed in leather or latex, many adorned with chains and slave collars.

Along with the usual array of whips, chains, cuffs, gags, dildos and sex toys, there was an entire section of BDSM furniture and restraining devices, as well as a huge selection of leather and fetish wear. The management had what they called a user-friendly policy, and they encouraged people to try out the equipment before they bought, though they drew the line at any actual scenes.

If he'd had more time, they could have spent the day in the place, as many fetish and BDSM enthusiasts did. Donovan would have enjoyed placing Jaime in the stocks and playfully smacking her shapely ass, or strapping her into the inversion chair and slowly tipping her until she was completely upside down, legs spread wide. Unfortunately, duty called at the clinic, so he led the wide-eyed and gaping young woman past the BDSM furniture and equipment to the clothing racks.

He moved along the aisles. "I was thinking something from this rack might fit the bill nicely," he said, stopping in front of the corsets. He looked through the items until he found what he was looking for. It was a mini-dress of soft black leather, the top half of which was a corset that laced up the front.

"This would look hot on you. Though still super sexy, it provides the full coverage you would want for the club. And look, it's got the garters built in." He took the dress from the rack and held it out, turning it so Jaime could see. "There's a nice long zipper up the back so it's easy to get on and off. What do you think?"

Jaime eyed the skimpy dress and nodded with approval. "I like it." She glanced around the store. "Do they have fitting rooms? Can I try it on?"

"Yeah. In the back. Let's grab some shoes and stockings too. I want to see the full effect." Donovan selected a pair of silky, sheer black stockings topped with lace while Jaime tried on several pairs of stiletto heels until she found a pair that fit.

They had to find a saleswoman to unlock a fitting room for Jaime. With pink hair and multiple tattoos, the girl appeared to be in her early twenties. "I'll just go in with you," she told Jaime. "You're going to need help getting that zipper up by yourself. Believe me, I know from personal experience."

Donovan settled down in a chair just outside the fitting rooms while he waited for Jaime to slip out of her blouse and jeans and reemerge transformed. When she finally stepped out of the fitting room, Donovan let out a low whistle of admiration. As the saleswoman nodded her approval, Jaime posed like a goddess, hands on her hips, her head cocked to the side. Several guys who had been passing by stopped and stared at her, their tongues literally hanging out of their mouths as they gaped at the slender beauty in her leather and lace.

Donovan had the sudden crazy impulse to smack the faces of the gawking men and order them to keep their eyes to themselves. He felt an unpleasant spasm in his chest and it took him a moment to identify the unfamiliar feeling.

Holy shit. He was jealous!

"How am I going to deal with all the horn dogs at the club once they get a load of you in that getup, eh, Mistress Jaime? You're going to be mobbed the minute you set foot in the club." He meant for his tone to be bantering, but wasn't sure he'd quite pulled it off.

Fortunately, Jaime just laughed. "No harder than me having to watch you dom all those gorgeous women every night for the adoring crowds. Good thing we're pros, huh?"

"Yeah. Good thing." Donovan glanced at his watch. "We better get going if I'm going to get to the clinic on time."

Jaime's grin faltered a little and Donovan felt bad, but he realized he had to put the brakes on whatever was happening before things skidded way out of control. In a voice that came out businesslike, even brusque, he instructed, "Just hand the things over the top of the door. I'll meet you at the checkout counter."

Jaime nodded, the smile completely gone now. "Yeah, sure."

They were quiet as they drove back to his neighborhood, letting the music from a jazz CD fill the car in lieu of conversation. Though he missed the easy warmth they'd shared on the drive over, he knew this was for the best. It wouldn't be fair to lead Jaime on or give her the wrong idea. The weekend had been great, but now it was over.

Traffic was even worse on the way home than it had been on the way there. "Shit," Donovan said, looking at his watch once he'd finally pulled into his driveway. "I'm going to be late for my shift." He climbed out of the car, walking around it toward Jaime, who stood clutching the bag containing her new outfit. "If I leave now I might just make it." He looked at Jaime. "Listen, would you mind locking up for me after you gather your things?" He held out the house key. "You can give it back tonight at the club."

Jaime took the key, frowning. "Sure. Or I could just wait here at the house till you get back later? We could go in to work together."

Donovan shook his head. "No, no. I'm sure you have stuff to do before the club opens. You've been away all weekend. I'll just see you later tonight." He took in the sudden hurt on her face and blew out a breath. "Hey, don't look like that." He reached for her, pulling her into his arms. "You were absolutely fantastic this weekend, Jaime. I'm so glad I won our bet. I hope you are too."

Jaime started to speak but Donovan stopped her by placing his mouth over hers. He kissed her long and deep, moving his tongue over her soft lips and into her mouth as he pulled her close. His cock rose against her body as he held her to him. If only he didn't have to go to the damn clinic today. If only he could spend a little longer pretending he was Jaime's real Master.

~*~

"So how was the weekend at the Master's place?" Annette was polishing glasses behind the counter when Jaime walked into the bar early that evening.

"What? How did you know I was there?" Jaime countered, taken completely by surprise by the question, though maybe in retrospect she shouldn't have been. After all, Gene and Donovan owned the club together. Maybe they were better friends than she'd realized.

Donovan's parting words had smacked her like cold water in the face. *I'm so glad I won our bet.* Was that really all it had been to him? Maybe Annette and Gene had been in on the bet. Maybe Donovan had given them a blow-by-blow account of the whole fucking weekend after he'd sent her away.

Annette, obviously unaware of the turmoil in Jaime's head or the tight knot in the pit of her stomach, replied, "Donovan must have turned off his cell phone for the weekend. He does that sometimes, so we weren't really worried. Anyway, Gene decided just to swing by Sunday night to drop off some tax papers. When he saw your car there, he decided it could wait." She flashed a grin and then continued, "Then we drove by this morning and your car was *still* there, so…" She paused and then waggled her eyebrows in a comically suggestive way. "Come on, you can tell me. Girl to girl. Out with it. Hold nothing back. My main question is, who dommed who?" Annette laughed.

When Jaime didn't join in, Annette sobered, hung the glass she'd been polishing and set down the cloth. Leaning over the bar, she put her hand over Jaime's. "What, honey? What is it? I was only joking around. I hope you didn't take offense. I've seen the sparks flying between you two ever since you started here. I figured it would just be a matter of time before you hooked up."

Jaime glanced around the barroom. Though Gene had told her she didn't need to show up much before nine, she was nearly an hour early. She hadn't wanted to knock around her apartment any longer. She'd spent the rest of the afternoon trying not to read too much into Donovan's abrupt dismissal of her, after the intensity of the weekend. She'd thought of calling or texting him, but after the strange way the morning had ended, she'd decided not to. Let him get in touch first and explain himself.

She'd looked at her cell phone at least a dozen times as the hours passed, staring at the blank screen as if it were a broken heart in her palm.

Had she misread the weekend so completely?

Not willing to share all this with Annette, Jaime asked instead, "Where's the new waitress?"

Annette withdrew her hand and reached for another glass to polish. "Suzanne is with Gene, doing some paperwork. I've already given her a quick refresher of her duties. She worked here for a few months a couple of years back. She did a good job, too, but she moved away. She'd been living down in LA for a while but had recently moved back up here. Talk about good timing! She actually called *us* to see if there was an opening. You excited about your new gig?"

Relieved Annette had changed the subject, Jaime nodded. "Yeah. I need your help with the zipper of my new outfit, if you have a minute."

Annette threw the dish towel over her shoulder and came around the side of the bar. "Sure. Let's go."

They walked together through the dungeon to the staff changing room. As they passed the bondage wheel, Jaime saw the image of herself, naked and bound, her arms and legs spread wide, the Master leaning toward her with those piercing blue eyes, a flogger in his hands. The image was so clear she had to blink twice until it disappeared.

Shaking her head, Jaime followed Annette into the staff changing room. She removed her blouse and jeans and took the sexy new dress off its satin-covered hanger.

"Nice," Annette remarked. "Is it new?"

Jaime nodded. "Donovan bought it for me this morning."

Annette lifted her eyebrows. "Did he now?"

After Annette had zipped Jaime into the snug corset dress, she sat on the bench, watching as Jaime rolled her stocking into place and attached the garters that hung from the hem. "You are going to turn some heads in that outfit, Mistress," she said in a wistful tone. "Almost makes me miss my professional Dominatrix days."

"You were a pro?" Jaime asked, momentarily forgetting her angst over the Master.

Annette nodded. "Sure was. That's how I met Gene. I used to rent dungeon space at The Vault. He was my best customer." She smiled fondly in recollection. "I knew he was in love with me before he did." She grinned. "But I kept it to myself for the longest time. Until I started falling in love back." Her grinned broadened. "As I'm sure you know, a kind of transference goes on sometimes in that kind of scene. Guys think they're in love with you, but really they just love what you can give them. You have to be very, very careful not to get that submissive devotion mixed up with love."

Jaime nodded, her angst returning. Was that what had been going on in Donovan's head? Did he think she wanted not the man, but only what he could give her? Was he just protecting himself?

Annette interrupted her thoughts, adding, "When we first started seriously dating, I kept up the pro Domme gig for a while. Gene was cool about it, because he knew there was no actual sex going on, but I found my heart just wasn't in it anymore. Truth to tell, I was burning out, even if Gene hadn't come into my life. I was ready to do something different. When he got the chance to buy this club, I was happy to give up my space at The Vault and sign on as barkeep, since that's what I did before becoming a pro Domme."

She smiled encouragingly at Jaime. "Don't get me wrong. It's a great gig, especially for someone single like you. No complications that way, you know? And there are tons of guys desperate to submit, and a lot fewer women, unfortunately, ready to take them in hand. If you're good at what you do, you'll have as many clients as you can handle."

Jaime slipped into her high heels and turned in front of the three-way mirror. "I'm a little nervous about my first night as a pro," she confessed. "I hope it works out."

"Oh, don't worry," Annette said. "You definitely look the part in that outfit. And, any personal attraction aside, Donovan wouldn't have agreed to hire you if he hadn't been impressed with your audition. You have what it takes. Just tap into your inner bitch and you'll be terrific." She laughed and Jaime laughed too, a little of the tightness inside her uncoiling.

Annette patted the bench. "Hey, sit down a minute. Tell me what's going on with you. Is it something with Donovan? I know him pretty well. He's a great guy but he can be pretty dense sometimes. He's a guy, after all, even if he is the Master." She laughed again, her dark eyes sparkling.

Jaime sat and sighed as she hunched over, catching her hands between her knees. "I don't really know what's going on, to tell you the truth. We had this bet, see." She paused, but then plunged on, suddenly desperate to confide in someone, especially someone who knew Donovan. "Donovan got it into his head that I'm secretly a sub, beneath my dominant exterior, as he calls it. He made me a bet that we would do a scene"—she felt herself coloring, but pushed on—"and if it affected me, you know, um, if it reached this secret submissive core he thought I possessed, then he would get to have me for forty-eight hours as his personal sex slave."

Annette snorted with laughter. "That's a good one. Leave it to Donovan to come up with something like that. What did you get if he lost the bet?"

"I'd have *him* as *my* personal sex slave."

"So, I take it you *lost* the bet? And you were *forced* to spend the weekend as his submissive sex slave?" Annette laughed again, shaking her head. "Between you and me, that sounds kind of like a win-win situation. I'd be willing to sub to the Master for a couple of days, and I *don't* have a secret submissive core, as you call it. I am dominant through and through. I mean, don't get me wrong, I love Gene to death, but Donovan Cartwright is seriously hot. A weekend with him would be just fine with me."

She leaned toward Jaime conspiratorially. "So, tell me, just between us girls. Was the Master as amazing in person as he is on stage? More importantly, did you have fun?"

"More than fun. It was amazing. It was sublime." Jaime hadn't meant to admit this quite so readily or so fervently, but it was true.

Annette cocked an eyebrow. "Sublime, huh? So what's the problem?"

When Jaime didn't immediately answer, Annette frowned and hit her forehead with the flat of her hand. "Oh, shit. What am I saying? This is Donovan we're talking about. *That's* the problem. You're falling for him, aren't you? I mean, *really* falling for him, not just riding the high of an amazing weekend."

"Yeah," Jaime admitted.

"And nobody warned you that Donovan Cartwright, while a lovely guy and a fabulous Dom, is genetically incapable of commitment. At least that's been my empirical observation in all the years I've known the guy."

"What?"

"Yep." Annette nodded soberly. "I guess it's both a gift and a curse. A gift because he's able to give of himself one-hundred percent, each and every time he does a scene. There's no conflict, imagined or otherwise, with someone waiting on her knees at home for the Master to return. This makes him great for the club, great for business. But a curse, too, because no one's ever been able to capture and tame his wild heart."

Jaime wiped away sudden tears with the back of her hand. She tried to take comfort from Annette's words. At least they made a kind of sense. Donovan hadn't been specifically rejecting her, Jaime. He was just a commitment-phobe who was genetically incapable of connecting with *anyone* on an intimate level. The tears fell faster, these thoughts offering little comfort.

"Hey," Annette said gently, putting her hand on Jaime's shoulder. "You've really fallen for the Master, huh?"

Miserably Jaime nodded. "Yeah. Stupid, huh?"

"No, not stupid. Entirely understandable."

Annette was quiet for a while, her hand still resting on Jaime's shoulder while Jaime forced her tears away. Suddenly Annette removed her hand and twisted to face Jaime.

"Genetics," she said solemnly, "can be altered."

Then she grinned.

# Chapter 13

"Ladies and gentlemen, it's my distinct pleasure to introduce you to Mistress Jaime, our new Mistress in residence here at The Bondage Wheel. Starting tomorrow evening she'll be taking private clients in the red room. You can sign up for fifteen to sixty minute sessions. The prices for her private services are listed in the red fliers on the bar and on the tables at the back." Gene was standing on the main stage in the dungeon, Jaime and Donovan on either side. Hoots and applause followed his announcement. All eyes were on Mistress Jaime, including Donovan's.

She looked better than fine, her hands confidently on her hips, the tops of her perfect round breasts bunched alluringly over the bone-stayed leather of her corset dress, her long, slender legs drawing the eye to her arched feet shod in the fuck-me stiletto heels. Donovan had a sudden fantasy of pushing Gene aside and striding directly up to Jaime. He would reach for her, slipping his hands into the tight corset and tugging her lush, creamy breasts free of their confines. He would lower his mouth and close his lips over her nipples, sucking each to a hard point before pushing her to her knees. He would show the guys who were practically salivating as they pressed close to the stage that this so-called Mistress belonged to *him*, the Master.

"Tonight, to give you a taste of Mistress Jaime's formidable talents, she has graciously agreed to do a scene with the Master." This pronouncement was greeted with more applause, the collective gaze finally shifting toward Donovan, who gave a small, theatrical bow. "With that," Gene said, glancing with a smile in Donovan's direction before looking again at the crowd, "I leave you to it. Have fun and remember our bywords when you scene, whether in public or private—safe, sane and consensual."

Gene moved to the back of the stage, as they'd previously planned for the upcoming scene, while Donovan moved to the center and gazed down at the audience, catching the eye of his chosen couple and smiling down at them. Congregated around the stage was the usual weekday crowd of about forty people. Fridays and Saturdays drew easily triple that number, many of them gawkers and dabblers who would stare, eyes wide, fists at their mouths, at the scandalous goings-on around them. Though he knew the weekend amateurs were good for business, Donovan actually preferred performing for what he perceived were the more serious players that came out on the weekdays.

He looked now at Jaime, who had moved closer to him on the stage. She was wearing more makeup than he was used to seeing on her—her lips painted a shiny, dark red, the golden-red fringe of her thick lashes now coated with black and accentuated with eyeliner. She looked hot, every inch a Mistress, powerful and in full control. She stared boldly back at him with those flashing green eyes, no hint of the girl who had slept so sweetly in his arms only the night before.

When he had arrived earlier that evening, he'd been a little nervous, not sure what she would expect now that the weekend was over and they would have to work together. He'd spent much of the afternoon and early evening alternating between daydreaming about the amazing time they'd spent together, and cursing himself for getting involved, if that's what he'd done, with a colleague. It had been a lark, a one-time thing, a way to prove his point beyond all doubt that more lay beneath Jaime's dominant exterior than she had heretofore been willing to admit.

But women so easily got the wrong idea. It wasn't their fault—they were just hardwired that way. They confused passion for love, and when you threw D/s in the mix, the lines were even easier to blur. He'd worried when he got to the club she might do something embarrassing like sink to her knees in front of him and wrap her arms around his thighs, resting her cool, soft cheek against him as she murmured her undying love and submission.

She had done no such thing.

In fact, she barely seemed to notice his arrival. Admittedly, he'd come in rather late, just before the club opened, his entrance timed to avoid any uncomfortable reunion between the two of them. He'd found her in the staff changing room. She'd been putting on her stage makeup, brushing the mascara wand over her lashes, her lips parted in concentration as she stared into the mirror.

His body had reacted without his mind's consent—his cock stiffening at the sight of her, his loins recalling the sweet, yielding warmth of her, his heart constricting in a way that was almost painful. He approached her from behind, deciding it wouldn't be such a terrible thing if she fell into his arms, lifting her face for a kiss, her eyes fluttering closed in anticipation.

But instead, upon catching sight of his image in the mirror, she'd only smiled, lifting her hand in a small wave. "Hey there," she'd said, not even turning around. "Glad you could make it."

For a moment he was taken aback. Where was the sweet, trembling girl he'd held in his arms only that morning? He'd quickly got hold of himself, however, relieved Jaime was taking things in stride. Her reaction, he'd told himself firmly, was the best he could possibly have hoped for. No complications, no recriminations, no expectations. The sub girl was gone, replaced by Mistress Jaime, and that was all to the good.

"Mary and Richard have volunteered to serve us tonight," Donovan now told the crowd surrounding the stage. "For those of you who don't know these two, Mary and Richard are both avowed subs who also happen to be happily married to each other. I've had the honor of working with them before in private sessions. Tonight will be their first public scene, so please welcome the couple."

The crowd parted amidst scattered applause as Mary and Richard, a trim pair in their mid-forties, ascended the stage stairs. Donovan had spied them when he'd first arrived at the dungeon, an idea springing into his head for Mistress Jaime's debut. They had readily agreed to the described scenario. When he'd consulted with Jaime, she, too, had agreed it would be a fun, if challenging, scene. "Just follow my lead," Donovan had told her. "I'll do the talking while on stage, though of course you should feel free to chime as you're comfortable in doing so. I know your primary gig is to take the private clients, but this will be a good introduction to our patrons."

"Don't worry, Donovan. I know my way around a public scene," she had reassured him, her tone haughty, though when he'd glanced at her face, her expression had been completely guileless.

Mary and Richard could have been brother and sister, both of them of medium height, with slight builds and closely cropped blond hair over sparkling blue eyes. Richard was wearing a black T-shirt and black jeans, black work boots on his feet. Mary was wearing a red silk dress with spaghetti straps, matching sheer red thigh high stockings and shiny red patent leather high heels. They both looked nervous but excited as they moved to the center of the stage.

"Strip," Donovan commanded. Without hesitation, Richard kicked off his boots, tugged his T-shirt from his pants and unzipped his jeans. Mary reached for the hem of her short dress and lifted it over her head, revealing her pale, slender body. Her nipples were pierced with gold hoops, her sex shaven smooth.

"Leave the shoes and stockings on, Mary," Jaime said, her voice low and sexy, but at the same time authoritative. Donovan had to agree the look was much sexier that way than if Mary had stripped completely naked. He nodded in approval toward Jaime, who lifted her chin and graced him with the ghost of a smile.

Once the couple was stripped down as instructed, Donovan pointed to the ground and they knelt side-by-side facing the audience, their hands behind their backs, their heads lowered submissively.

Donovan again turned toward the audience. "Richard has agreed to be suspended, upside down, while his lovely wife pays proper homage to his manhood." Amidst the audience's enthusiastic reception to this news, Donovan continued. "I know from experience that both these subs like a little challenge." He chuckled, "No, make that a lot of challenge, and we wouldn't want to disappoint them. So tonight Mary's hands will be bound behind her back while she services her husband, and Mistress Jaime and I will add a little, uh, incentive to the pair with our whips."

He bent down, tapping each sub's shoulder. They rose and followed him to the pulleys that were suspended from a thick beam in the ceiling over the stage. Richard lay obediently on the floor while Donovan and Jaime closed the sturdy cuffs that were attached to the spreader bar around his ankles and secured the bar to the pulley mechanism. They affixed thick cuffs with large D rings around his thighs and smaller cuffs around his wrists, which they clipped to the rings on the thigh cuffs to keep Richard's arms in place while he was suspended.

When they were done, Donovan nodded toward Gene, who was waiting by the pulley winch at the back wall. Gene turned the winch slowly while Donovan spotted Richard. The spreader bar lifted, pulling Richard's legs up into the air. Gene continued turning the winch until Richard was at the proper height, his head a foot or so above the floor, his already erect cock level with Mary's chin.

Donovan had Mary place her arms behind her back, one forearm horizontally over the other. He wrapped soft but sturdy rope around her wrists and forearms, tying the ends in a simple knot that could be quickly released.

Leaving the bound pair, Donovan went to the whip rack on the side of the stage to select two floggers, but he was stopped by Jaime's small, pretty hand on his. "I'll pick my own, thanks," she informed him quietly. Donovan nodded, watching as she chose a small but lethal single tail. As soon as she selected it, Donovan silently agreed it was the better choice for Richard.

They returned to center stage where their charges waited, naked and bound. Donovan looked out over the dungeon. Not a single private scene was in play. Every person in the place was at the stage. Even Annette and Suzanne had come in from the bar to watch. The place was silent with expectation, kinetic energy zinging through the air.

Mistress Jaime stood behind Richard, lightly stroking his skin with the leather tail of her whip. Donovan stood behind Mary and touched the top of her head. In a voice designed to carry, he said, "Mary, your task is to make your husband come. You will need to be very focused on what you are doing. Don't let the flogger distract you. And you, Richard, use the pain from the single tail to get you where you need to go. The longer it takes, the more intense the whipping will become."

He pushed Mary's head gently forward between Richard's spread legs. "Begin," he commanded.

Mary ducked her head, closing her mouth over her husband's shaft. Her task was made more difficult without the use of her hands, but Donovan knew from experience Mary was very accomplished at this particular task, hands or no. He began to flog her gently, swishing the leather tresses over her back and ass as she took Richard's cock deep into her throat.

Donovan's eyes kept flitting to Jaime as he flogged the woman in front of him. Though it was just a memory, he could almost hear Jaime's breathy, sensual cries as leather met skin, and his cock nudged against his thigh as he recalled Jaime naked and panting at his feet.

The sudden, sharp snap of Mistress Jaime's whip made Richard wince and drew several gasps from onlookers. She stared at Donovan as if the whip had been intended for him, a fire glittering in her green eyes. The image of the sexy, submissive slave girl he'd possessed for forty-eight hours evaporated like mist against a burning sun.

Forcing himself to focus on the scene before him, Donovan matched Mistress Jaime's intensity with his flogger, flicking his wrist and catching Mary's small ass beneath her bound arms with the full force of his stroke. Mary, deeply masochistic and highly sexualized, moaned against her husband's cock and actually stuck out her ass to receive the sting of the leather.

Donovan glanced again at Jaime, his eyes drawn to her in spite of himself. She was focused on Richard, her lips parted in concentration as she moved in a sensual dance behind him. The air cracked with the sound of her whip as she expertly flicked the single tail over the suspended sub's ass, thighs and shoulders. As if feeling Donovan's gaze on her, Jaime looked up suddenly and their eyes met. Just as suddenly she looked away, but not before he saw something of the yearning sub girl he'd left behind only that morning.

Not sure if her look had been real or a product of his imagination, Donovan refocused on Mary, catching her ass and thighs again and again in the stinging embrace of the flogger, watching as her skin reddened to match the sheer red stockings hugging her pretty legs. Mary was a wonderful submissive, highly trained and deeply responsive. Donovan had always enjoyed his sessions with the submissive couple. Having Jaime there simply added to the intensity, he told himself. *Just stay in the moment.* They were performing together and the dynamic between them was good. It was all good.

Richard began to moan, his breath coming in a rapid staccato of pleasure and pain as one woman sucked his cock while the other whipped his ass. All at once he stiffened, his hands clenching into fists at his thighs, his neck straining.

"Please, Mistress, may I come!" he shouted, as his wife continued dutifully bobbing between his legs, in spite of being steadily flogged from behind. Donovan felt a sudden and, he knew, irrational twinge of jealousy and annoyance that Richard, his longtime client, had asked not him, the Master, but rather, Jaime, for permission to come.

"You may," Mistress Jaime replied in a clear, ringing tone. She continued to whip the now shuddering man as he shot his load down his wife's throat. The room burst into spontaneous shouts of approval and applause. Once Richard's spasms had died down, Jaime and Donovan lowered their whips and smiled at one another.

Donovan nodded toward Gene, who had remained standing near the winch in case of emergency. Gene lowered the naked man slowly while Donovan and Jaime helped Richard into position on the ground and then quickly released his cuffs. Finally Donovan turned back to Mary, who was kneeling on the stage like the well-trained sub she was, her head bowed. Donovan stroked her hair and she leaned into his hand like a kitten as she looked up at him with adoring eyes.

Donovan released her arms and helped her to feet, giving her a quick hug and a pat on her bare ass before sending her into the embrace of her husband, who stood naked and grinning, his arms open to receive her.

Gene had returned to center stage. "There'll be another show at midnight, and this time the Master will be taking volunteers. Meanwhile, have fun."

Again the place erupted into applause. Jaime looked at Donovan, and once more he could have almost sworn he saw the longing there. But before he could respond, she had turned away and was beaming down at the audience as several men began to chant, "Mistress Jaime! Mistress Jaime!"

Gene turned to Donovan and nudged him in the ribs. "I think this is the start of something big, partner. That scene was fucking stellar. The subs were great, but it was the energy between you and Jaime that really heated things up. Whatever it is that's going on between the two of you, keep it up, dude. Keep it up."

~*~

Jaime sat at the bar, a glass of chilled grapefruit juice and vodka over crushed ice untouched in front of her. She wanted to go home with Donovan and snuggle into his arms in his bed, but he had disappeared shortly after the stage scene, swallowed by the usual crowd of hangers-on and admirers.

Though it had been tough, she was proud of how she'd comported herself throughout the night with respect to the Master. And she was grateful to Annette for her excellent advice in that regard. Left to her own devices, Jaime might have turned around when Donovan had entered the changing room and thrown herself headlong into his arms. Worse, she might have demanded to know why the bastard hadn't called her or texted her after they'd just spent the most amazing two days of her life together. Had it really meant so little to him? Was he really so shallow as that? Had it all just been one big game to him?

Jaime wanted to talk to Annette, who was busy pouring drinks. Even if Annette had been free, Jaime found herself surrounded by a host of men and some women too, all of them eager for her attention. She'd already booked a dozen private sessions in the red room for later in the week, and from the steady clamor around her, she figured she'd have another dozen scheduled before the night was over. It was kind of hard to get her head around the idea that she was going to be paid for doing what she loved — what she'd done for free back in the city for all those years.

No question, the stage scene with Donovan had been electric. Mary and Richard were amazing, but beyond that, in spite of her confusion over the past hours since they'd parted, Jaime had felt a powerful connection with the Master on stage. It was as if they'd been one person, one entity, as they'd dommed the submissive couple, each somehow sensing not only what the subs needed, but also what each other was doing or about to do, as if they'd practiced and choreographed the scene to perfection, as if they'd been doing it for years.

When the audience had burst into thunderous cheering and applause, after the initial thrill Jaime had wanted to throw herself into Donovan's arms. Or, like Mary, she had wanted to sink to her knees and wait to feel his hand on her head, like a benediction. Fortunately, she'd caught herself in time, forcing herself to focus on the cheering audience instead of the commitment-phobe standing beside her.

"Men like that are like wild horses," Annette had told her earlier that evening. "One false move and they run. If you try to break them with what they perceive is a saddle, they'll throw you to the ground and leave you in the dust."

"I just don't get it," Jaime had said, running her hands through her short hair as she sat beside Annette on the bench. "He wasn't like that. For the entire weekend he was totally focused on me. Like I was the only person on earth, and he acted like that was fine with him, like it was perfect. How could he go from that to completely dismissing me within a matter of hours?" She had felt her eyes tearing up and rapidly blinked away the tears. No way in hell was she going to cry on the night of her debut as Mistress Jaime.

Annette had patted her shoulder. "First of all, it helps to remember that Donovan is an idiot." When Jaime looked askance at her, Annette laughed, adding, "A wonderful idiot, but still an idiot, at least in the ways of the heart. I don't doubt that everything he said and did this weekend was done with utter and complete sincerity. Whatever else Donovan might be, he's definitely *not* full of shit."

Annette had paused, staring for a moment into the middle distance before continuing. "I think the crux of the matter is fear. Donovan's got a kind of charisma that attracts women across the board. In the San Francisco BDSM scene he's become something of a legend. We have a much higher female clientele here at The Bondage Wheel than your average BDSM club, and Donovan Cartwright is the reason. All that attention can go to a guy's head. He's used to just pointing and the chosen woman will fall swooning at his feet, metaphorically speaking. When he actually bumps up against the real thing, against the potential for love, he's too blind, or too scared, to actually realize what he's got. But again, remember the wild horse analogy. If you want to coax him back into your arms, you need to take your time. You need to approach him carefully, cautiously, even indifferently. *That* will be a lot more effective in the end. If you have the patience for it, that is."

Jaime wasn't sure she did have the patience. It pissed her off that the first man she'd fallen for, really fallen for, in years, was now running scared as if she were some kind of desperate woman sending out marriage vibes or whatever the hell it was he was afraid of. She'd been judged and sentenced without any trial for a crime she hadn't committed.

Yeah, the weekend had been stunning. It had opened up a whole new world of possibility for Jaime, a world she'd never even entertained until Donovan had shown her its power and potential. Though she'd been frightened at first by the intensity of what he offered and her own reaction to it, she remained intrigued, even eager to continue the exploration with Donovan.

But Jaime Heller was not one to sit home alone by the phone, weeping and waiting for some man. If Donovan was too stupid, too timid, too whatever the hell he was to realize that what they'd shared that weekend had gone way past just satisfying some bet, then he didn't deserve her.

Jaime swiveled on her barstool and focused on the small crowd of men still hovering around her. They all smiled as she graced them with her attention, wanting to know where she'd been hiding, and if she had her own dungeon, and what her rates were. One especially handsome man, an African American with dark soulful eyes and very white teeth, sat on the empty stool beside her and said in a low, sexy voice, "Tell me, Mistress Jaime, do you play the other side? While I was watching you on the stage, I had this incredible image of you suspended by your wrists in my dungeon, your lovely green eyes wide with fear and anticipation as you watched me sharpen my knives." He put his hand on her thigh. "Have you ever experimented with blood play? It can be very, very powerful."

Jaime swallowed hard, startled by this abrupt turn in the conversation. She started to assure the man in no uncertain terms that she had zero interest in blood play, especially if he expected her to be on the receiving end. But at that moment, Donovan strode into the bar, several women trailing behind him like a pack of puppies. As Donovan approached, Jaime turned her focus entirely to the man beside her.

Reaching out, she touched his leather-clad knee. "No," she said earnestly as she gazed into his liquid brown eyes. "I never have. Tell me more."

# Chapter 14

Donovan put his hand lightly on Jaime's shoulder, trying not to glare at the guy who was leaning way too far into her personal space.

It had taken him nearly a half hour to extricate himself from the usual cluster of admirers who always materialized after a show, along with a handful of subs, both male and female, who wanted to know if they could be the volunteers for the midnight show. He was leaning toward selecting Gina, a statuesque brunette who, he knew from experience, enjoyed extreme bondage and was quite limber.

He felt bad for leaving Jaime alone for so long. He knew how exciting your first stage show could be. They had been an incredible team up there, their shared energy powerful. Jaime, new to the experience, needed to decompress. Maybe he would suggest they slip out for a little while to a nearby pub, or at least snag a private table at the back of the bar.

It wasn't like whatever had started between them had to be over. Now that he saw how easily she'd adjusted to their working together at the club, maybe they could still be weekend play partners. After all, they had barely begun to scratch the surface of her submissive potential in the two days they'd been together. Jaime was like a tight, perfect rosebud, poised and ready to bloom. Who better than he to oversee and nurture that blossoming?

It was decided. He would ask her to join him for a quick drink at the pub next door. Maybe on the way he would push her gently but firmly against an alley wall, pinning her there as he bent down to kiss her, just to remind her of the weekend, of who was really in control.

Jaime swiveled slowly toward him, a look of casual surprise on her face at seeing him. Her hand, he noticed with annoyance, remained on the knee of the guy she had been talking to. It was, Donovan now realized, Brent Underwood, a regular at the club. Underwood never tired of telling Donovan he was an MD, like Donovan was supposed to be super impressed by that. The arrogant prick.

"Oh, hey there," Jaime said breezily, as if they hadn't just spent an amazing weekend together and then conducted one of the best shows in the club's history together. "What's up?"

Donovan stiffened, her distracted response hitting him like a slap in the face. What had he wanted? For her to fall to her knees and kiss his boots? The pub, the scene against the wall—he realized now he was fantasizing about something that would not come to pass. With her body language and her dismissive tone, Jaime was stating loud and clear that she wasn't interested.

He forced himself to smile back and gave a noncommittal shrug. "Just checking in. I was thinking maybe you'd care to join me for the second show at midnight. I was planning some bondage and suspension action. I already have one volunteer selected."

Donovan hadn't realized he was going to make that offer until it was out of his mouth. He hadn't expected the powerful connection he'd felt on the stage with Jaime during the scene with Mary and Richard. He had to admit she'd been flawless in her execution, and had even made some better choices than he might have if left entirely on his own.

Still, he was the Master. He'd spent years honing his craft and making his name in the San Francisco BDSM club scene. He was bestowing quite an honor on this newcomer by asking her to join him for the second show. If nothing else, he reasoned to himself, it would be a good way to get her out of Underwood's clutches. The bastard was staring much too intently at Jaime, his eyes moving insolently over her body as if he owned her.

To Donovan's dumbfounded dismay, Jaime shook her head. "Thanks for the offer, but I don't think so." She tapped the small, leather-bound notebook on the bar in front of her and offered an apologetic shrug. "I've already booked enough sessions to fill the next week, and since I won't be starting in my formal capacity until tomorrow, Gene said it was fine if I left early tonight."

She put her hand lightly on Donovan's arm, her touch sending an electric current of desire directly to his cock. "Maybe once I'm more settled in my new role as Mistress in residence we can do another show together." Jaime's smile pierced Donovan's heart like a barb as she pulled her hand away. She swiveled back to the man beside her, Donovan apparently dismissed. "You were saying, Master Brent?"

*What* the hell had just happened?

~*~

Jaime stood under the shower spray in her tiny apartment long after she'd finished washing her body and her hair, just letting the hot water splash over her. Last night had been miserable, going against all her instincts in following Annette's advice and leaving the club before midnight. How her heart had leapt when she'd turned on her barstool to find Donovan standing behind her. She'd known it before she even turned around, his touch instantly heating her skin, his scent perking her nipples and soaking her cunt.

When he'd invited her to do another show with him, she'd been dying to accept, thrilled at the offer, aware they would need to meet beforehand to plan it out. But through it all, Annette's warning words had echoed in her mind. Just before they'd gone on stage, Annette had pulled Jaime aside.

"Remember," Annette had said, "all is fair in love and war, and right now, though you may not realize it, you're engaged in both. No matter what Donovan does or says, you say *no*. Do it sweetly, do it kindly, but *do* it. Tonight is the first tactical move in our battle. You're setting up the field so he understands you are not the usual sub girl he's come to expect, with her heart on her sleeve, waiting and praying for the Master to notice her."

When Jaime had protested, Annette had crossed her arms firmly and stared Jaime down with all the power and persuasion she could muster, which was considerable. "You are Mistress Jaime, and don't you forget it. The weekend was great, but, like the Master, you're moving on. Donovan is so used to women throwing themselves at him, he won't know what hit him. Trust me, no one ever turns down the Master. You'll be the first, and, if we play our cards right, the last."

Still, Jaime had been so tempted by Donovan's offer. It would be the perfect way to get him alone, without seeming at all desperate. But Annette had been standing right there on the other side of the bar when Donovan had approached, flashing warning daggers at Jaime with her eyes. Though it had nearly killed Jaime to do it, she'd turned the Master down, and the hurt in his face had been both heartbreaking and thrilling. Had she done the right thing? God, she hoped so.

Just as Jaime turned off the shower she heard her cell ringing. Grabbing a towel, she dashed from her tiny bathroom to the bedroom and grabbed the phone, her heart soaring. Donovan!

But it wasn't Donovan. *Betsy Hanover* showed on the screen. A sudden wave of guilt surged through Jaime, and she took the call. "Betsy! Hey, how are you? I've been meaning to call."

"I'm doing fine. How's it going on the West Coast? Tell me everything. Spare no detail. Has Mistress Jaime taken them all by storm?"

Jaime laughed. "Well, yes, as a matter fact!" Should she confide in Betsy about her amazing experience as Donovan's temporary sub girl? Should she admit she had fallen head over feet for a commitment-phobe? Betsy would tell her to cut the guy loose and find a real man, a man would knew what he had. Not quite ready to have that particular conversation, Jaime instead told Betsy all about the club, and her rise from waitress to Mistress in residence.

During Jaime's description of the stage show the night before, Betsy interrupted, "I've heard about Donovan Cartwright, though I never met him personally. He's got a great reputation as a trainer. You might learn a thing or two from the guy."

"What do you mean? I know what I'm doing, thank you very much." Jaime found herself bristling at the implication she needed lessons in domination.

"Don't get your panties in a bunch, sweetheart." Betsy laughed. "I'm not talking about Dominatrix training. Remember our conversation before you left? About you exploring your submissive side? He might be a good person to approach in that regard. He could help you explore those impulses you apparently continue to deny."

Jaime was silent, temporarily speechless.

"You still there?" Betsy finally said.

"Yes," Jaime whispered.

"What is it? I've known you long enough now. You're keeping something from me. Come on, spill the beans."

"Well," Jaime hesitated. "It's kind of complicated. It's a long story—"

"That's all right," Betsy interjected. "I've got all the time in the world. Tell me."

And so Jaime did, telling her about the bet, about the amazing weekend, and about Donovan's sudden withdrawal. After crowing a little about her gut feel regarding Jaime's inherently submissive nature, Betsy, as Jaime had feared, derided Donovan for having his head lodged firmly up his ass, asserting that men like that didn't deserve the women who loved them. "Wait a minute," she interrupted herself. "*Do* you love him?"

"Yes," Jaime admitted before she had a chance to censor herself.

"Then don't listen to me. What the hell do I know, anyway? Find a way to let him know. Find a way to reach him."

The waiter set down their plates, asked if they needed anything else, and left them alone. Jaime was glad she'd agreed to Annette's invitation to lunch at Café Rose, located down the block from the club. Though the day was sunny, Jaime pulled her sweater around her shoulders, still not used to the wind and mild temperatures of San Francisco, even though it was the end of June.

Jaime told Annette about Betsy's call, and her advice toward the end of their conversation.

Annette remained firm. "Betsy doesn't know Donovan like I do. Trust me, last night you handled it, or should I say him, brilliantly," Annette reassured her.

Jaime shook her head, still not entirely convinced. "I don't know," she said. "I don't like to play games like that. When I feel something for someone, which doesn't happen very often, I like to let them know. I mean, shit, I'm twenty-seven, not seventeen. I've been in love exactly twice before this, and not that I'm looking to get married or anything, but I'm not getting any younger."

Annette threw back her head and laughed. "Talk to me when you're pushing forty, babe. Gene and I didn't even meet until I was thirty-six to his thirty-three. You're still a spring chicken."

Jaime offered a rueful smile. "I guess it's relative. All I can say is I haven't felt like this in years. No, make that ever. I've never felt such a strong, immediate connection with someone. And the crazy thing is, the tragic thing really, is he's all wrong for me. Even if he wasn't a genetically-impaired commitment-phobe or whatever you called him, Donovan and I could never work out. We're both dominants. I know people say you can be a switch, but I don't buy it. You're one thing or the other. You can't just change your wiring, just like you can't be straight one day and gay the next."

As had happened at least a dozen times since Donovan had sent her away, tears flooded Jaime's eyes and she brushed them angrily away. What the hell was happening to her? She had never been a crier, but since she'd met Donovan, or no, make that since he'd ended things so abruptly the morning before, she couldn't seem to keep the tears at bay.

Who was she kidding? She knew what was wrong—she was in love with a man who was afraid to love her back, and even if he did, they had, by definition of their kink, no future together.

If she had expected comfort from Annette as she wiped at her tears, she didn't get it. Annette was grinning at her and shaking her head. "Kiddo, you're okay. Maybe a little confused, but okay. Come on, dry those tears." She waited while Jaime dabbed at her eyes with her napkin, before continuing, "I'm going to explain something to you, but first, eat your sandwich—you'll feel better. Go on, take a bite. I'll wait."

In spite of herself, Jaime laughed. "Bossy, aren't you?" she quipped.

Annette grinned. "Just ask Gene."

Jaime picked up her sandwich and took a bite, not really tasting it. "Okay. Go on," she said, suddenly happy in spite of everything as she realized she had a new friend, her first real friend in a long time. "Enlighten me, oh wise one."

Annette took a long drink of her iced tea and set it down with a regal nod. "Okay, here's the thing, Jaime. You said you can't be gay one day and straight the next, but I disagree. In fact, my theory, which I've seen born out countless times over the years, is that no one is one-hundred percent gay or one-hundred percent straight. Society wants to stick us in neat little slots, but human nature doesn't work that way. People are attracted along a continuum, some more skewed toward being straight, some toward gay, most somewhere in the middle, whether or not they ever allow themselves to feel, much less explore, their orientation."

She took another bite of her sandwich and then continued. "Same way in the BDSM scene, though I agree with you, folks tend to be more hardwired in one direction or the other, but there are times when someone who is primarily dominant has the urge to submit. By the same token, a primarily submissive person can be quite dominant, with the right person or in the right situation. Some of the most sadistic players I ever met were submissive to their primary partner."

Jaime nodded. "Betsy used to say the same thing. 'When you give a sub girl a whip to play with, watch out.'"

Annette laughed. "Yep. And the converse is also true. Back when I was a pro Domme, I had a number of clients who exuded power in their daily lives. These were professional power junkies who ran Fortune 500 companies, but they were more than happy during our sessions to wear my collar and kiss my feet. Not only happy, they needed it. It fulfilled a part of their nature that was subjugated and denied the rest of the time."

She leaned forward, her tone earnest. "Then there's you, Jaime. You fit into that profile, but in a more direct way. You define yourself as dominant in the scene, but who are you really? What moves you? What gets your heart racing and, if you'll pardon my French, your pussy soaking? Is it the look in a man's eye when you've got his balls in one hand and a whip in the other?" Annette laughed. "No wait, that's me we're talking about."

She sobered quickly, adding, "Seriously though, I could be all wrong, but I've been watching you and listening to what you've said about your experience with Donovan this weekend. These are not the words or feelings of a hardcore dominant. It's quite possible, Ms. Heller, that you are in fact a submissive in Domme's clothing." She grinned, adding, "Which isn't to say you aren't a kickass Domme. But I have a feeling that might be your vocation, while submission is your passion. And Donovan has been the one to unlock that passion, am I right?"

While Jaime struggled to take in what Annette was saying with her brain, her gut knew instantly that she was right. The realization was at once shocking and a relief, as if she were at last ready to embrace who she'd been all along.

Something made Jaime look up at that moment, as if someone had called her name. She stared across the street, her body registering what she saw before her brain could kick in. Her heart began to pound wildly. "Shit!" she said breathlessly. "That's Donovan across the street. He's looking at us! He's waving!"

Annette dropped her napkin on the table and stood, waving back in his direction. "Ah, the bait worked, and the fly is now approaching our honey."

"What?" Jaime's eyes remained glued to the man, who was standing at the traffic light with a dozen other people, waiting for it to change so he could safely cross the busy street. She pulled her gaze away long enough to glance sharply at Annette. "What're you talking about?"

Annette laughed. "I set him up. Last night after you left, he and Gene were at the bar. I overheard him say he might give you a call. Just to discuss a possible joint show for later in the week, he said. Seeing an excellent opportunity, I leaned right over the bar and informed him you were having lunch with Brent at Café Rose at two o'clock today. In an Oscar worthy performance, he shrugged and said oh-so-casually, 'You don't say?'"

"You said that?" Jaime squealed.

"I sure did. And just to make sure he got the point, I added that you seemed to be quite taken with the guy."

In spite of herself, Jaime laughed. "I can't believe you did that! I would never agree to lunch with a guy I just met. And certainly not with Master Brent, who was entirely too full of himself."

"You know that, and I know that, but the Master doesn't know that. And look." She gestured with her chin toward Donovan, who had crossed the street and was walking rapidly now in their direction with a determined stride. "Here he comes, ready to challenge Master Brent to a duel."

She turned toward Jaime, speaking rapidly. "Now listen carefully. I know you don't like to play games, and hopefully this will be one of the last ones you play, but don't fuck this up. Master Brent had something come up, so you asked me instead. You don't have to pretend to have feelings for the guy, but don't let Donovan off the hook too easily. He needs to figure out all by himself that he wants you. Think wild mustang. You can hold out the lump of sugar, but he has to come to you. You move too fast now, and he'll bolt. Got it?"

Jaime looked at Donovan approaching. He was wearing faded blue jeans that fit him perfectly, hugging his muscular thighs, but not too tight down the leg. As he got closer she could see snakes curling around his biceps beneath the short sleeve of his red T-shirt. He wore sunglasses, his sensuous mouth compressed in a thin line, though without seeing his eyes, she couldn't tell if he was angry or just nervous.

He slowed as he got closer and finally stopped in front of them. Jaime's heart was beating so hard she wondered if the others could hear it. She forced a casual smile as she looked up at him, shading her eyes with her hand.

Annette spoke first. "Well, hey there, Mr. Cartwright. What a small world. You had your lunch yet?" She pulled out a chair, waving for him to sit.

Donovan took off his glasses and looked from Jaime to Annette and back to Jaime. Then he looked past them at the other tables, a question on his face. Annette and Jaime exchanged a quick glance, Annette smirking, an *I told you so* expression on her face.

"Looking for someone?" Annette asked in an exaggeratedly innocent tone.

"You said—" Donovan began, before catching himself. He took the chair Annette had pulled out.

"I said Jaime and Brent were meeting for lunch. Unfortunately he got called into the hospital, poor bastard." She turned to Jaime with a guileless smile.

"I'm so glad you called me take his place, Jaime. I have a feeling we're going to be the best of friends."

The waiter arrived, a menu in hand. "Would you like to order something, sir?" he asked.

Donovan, who still looked confused, shook his head. "No, thanks. I'll just have a beer. Something on tap."

The waiter rattled off half a dozen options and Donovan selected one. He turned to Jaime. "So, you get a good night's rest? You sure were missed last night." By whom, he didn't say, but he was gazing at her with intense earnestness, as if she were the only person in the world.

Jaime nodded, not mentioning she'd tossed and turned for over an hour before finally deciding to masturbate to calm down, and certainly not mentioning the fantasies that unspooled in her head as she touched herself involved the Master, front and center.

Annette pulled her cell phone from her jacket pocket and stared down at it, shaking her head. "Gene's texting me. He needs me. I swear to god, I don't know how he survived before I took him in hand. He can't do a thing without me." She laughed affectionately and stood, dropping some bills onto the table. "You'll forgive me if I leave abruptly? Now that you have each other to keep you company?"

She was so convincing that Jaime wasn't even sure if she was making it up or not. Jaime glanced at

Donovan, who was smiling. "No problem. Gene needs you." He waved his hand. "Go on. I'll make sure Jaime gets home. I'm parked the next block over."

"That's okay," Jaime said, suddenly enjoying the power of her position. "I drove my own car." She glanced at her watch and used the tone she employed with her sub boys. "I still have a few minutes though. I'll stay while you drink your beer."

# Chapter 15

"So, Master Brent, huh?" Donovan said with exaggerated casualness. He raised his beer to his lips and drank as he appraised Jaime over the top of the glass. "I don't really see you with that guy."

"Oh?" Jaime lifted her lips into a small smile. "Who do you see me with?"

*Me,* Donovan started to say, before catching himself.

Though he'd thought of little but Jaime and Master Fucking Brent since the night before, Donovan had promised himself he wouldn't give the slightest hint that he cared what Jaime did with another man. He couldn't stand that kind of needy, possessive behavior in a woman, and had no intention of exhibiting it himself.

Yet he couldn't deny when he arrived at the café and saw, not the arrogant MD, but Annette at the table with Jaime, he'd nearly cried with relief. At that moment he couldn't pretend to himself any longer that he didn't care who Jaime hung out with, that she didn't matter more to him than any other of his casual submissive play partners. He'd had to physically restrain himself from pulling Jaime into his arms so he could kiss every inch of her face.

Instead, somehow keeping up the Mr. Cool façade, he'd agreed to join them for a quick beer, especially pleased when Annette suddenly needed to vacate the premises. Talk about good timing. Now he was alone with the girl he hadn't been able to get out of his head since their amazing weekend together. He would feel her out—see where she was with this Master Brent character—and take it from there. He would start with something innocuous, like if she got a good night's sleep, and try from that to determine if she'd slept alone or in another man's arms.

Her nod, however, hadn't provided the information he'd been seeking. Mr. Cool forgotten, Donovan found himself blurting, "Are you really seeing that jackass, Master Brent?"

Jaime, who had been sipping her iced tea, sputtered into her drink. Wiping her face with her napkin, she set down her glass and peered at him with a confused expression. "I'm sorry, what did you just say?"

Embarrassed at his outburst, which had come out of nowhere, Donovan tried to backtrack. "Oh, you know. I mean, uh, I saw you talking to him last night. Then you had to leave early. From the way you were ogling each other, I thought it was a reasonable assumption that you might leave together. Annette said you were having lunch with him today so…"

Jaime frowned, a *what-the-fuck* look on her face. She glared at him for a beat and then two. But she didn't deny it.

*So it was true. God damn it.*

Jaime cut short Donovan's rising ire by suddenly pronouncing, "I'm sorry. I can't do this."

What the hell was going on? *She* was the one who was upset? Donovan tilted his head as he looked at her, trying to rein in the jumble of emotions wrecking havoc in his head. "Can't do what?"

Jaime rubbed her hands over her face and sighed. "I can't keep playing this game. It's just—silly. I mean, I know Annette's heart is totally in the right place. But this just isn't how I operate."

"I'm sorry. You've lost me. What does Annette's heart have to do with anything?"

Color rose suddenly into Jaime's cheeks. "Well, if you want to know, Annette's been busy playing matchmaker behind the scenes."

Fury rose in a sudden bitter rush in Donovan's chest. How could Annette betray him like that? "Annette's trying to match you with Brent Underwood? Is she nuts? I thought she was my friend, for god's sake."

Jaime laughed, her cheeks still pink, her green eyes suddenly sparkling. "No, not Master Brent and me. *You* and me. She's been coaching me on how to tame wild horses."

Donovan shook his head. "Okay, now I have *no* idea what you're talking about. Where do horses come into this, other than Brent, who can be a horse's ass, no offense." He forced a laugh at his own admittedly rather weak joke, though he remained perplexed and angry.

Jaime took a deep breath and blew it out. "Okay," she said. "First I'll clear up something for you. While Master Brent seems like a decent guy, I'm not interested in him, not in the least. And frankly," some of the anger edged its way back into her face, "I can't believe you'd think I'm that fickle—after what you and I shared this weekend."

Despite himself, Donovan felt some of the tightness in his chest ease, though he remained unclear as to what was really going on. "So, wait," he said. "Why were you having lunch with him then? I don't get it."

"I *wasn't!*" Jaime's tone was exasperated. "Annette just floated that out there for bait, and you apparently swallowed it."

Now it was Donovan's turn to flush. He felt manipulated. Worse, he felt foolish. Why would Annette have done such a thing?

"Here's the thing," Jaime continued. "Annette has it in her mind that you're like a wild horse when it comes to women. You don't like to feel, to continue the metaphor, corralled. You need for it to be your idea when you want to be with a woman, and if she makes it her idea first, you feel hemmed in and you bolt. So she's been counseling me on how to be a horse whisperer and trick you into wanting me by offering lumps of sugar without seeming to. She's been teaching me to play it cool with the Master."

She reached over, placing her soft hand on his, her eyes flashing. "I've been doing my damnedest to pretend I didn't really mind that you just sent me packing yesterday morning after the most amazing forty-eight hours I'd ever spent with another human being. I've been trying to pretend you aren't the most exciting man I've ever met, and that you haven't opened a whole new world for me that I want to continue to explore with you."

She pulled her hand away and shrugged, her face suddenly closing. "Look, I'm sorry, I tried it her way, and even if it's working—if it got you here by artifice and feminine wiles—it's just not my style. I'm going to lay it out for you, and if you can't handle the truth, then so be it." She paused, as if daring him to contradict her, but Donovan stayed silent, still trying to process what she was saying, and his part in it.

Jaime's voice grew more determined, "I'm not saying I want to marry you, Donovan. I'm not saying I want to own you or be owned by you. I'm just saying I don't like to be treated like a one-night stand, and then have to pretend that how you behaved didn't hurt and confuse me. I'm saying I want to continue where we left off without having to worry I'm going to scare you away by expressing honest feelings. If that's a strike against me, so be it. This is who I am. Take it or leave it."

Donovan stared at the strong woman beside him, who was gazing back at him with a look of resigned defiance. And suddenly he felt as if he was in a movie, and the camera had moved in for a close-up, the world shrinking to this one moment in time, everything and everyone else falling away.

He realized in that one moment that for all of his adult life he'd been doing just exactly what Annette had accused him of—running at the first sign of real intimacy, scared to death of... Of what? Of being loved? Of being truly happy? Or of losing that love and ending up lonelier than when he'd started? He honestly didn't know.

All he knew was he wanted this woman sitting across from him like he'd never wanted anyone else. And hadn't he known that since the moment he'd contrived the bet so he could get her into his dungeon and into his bed? Yet even then, before he'd given them or her a chance, he'd already begun to push her away, at least in his head. The instant things threatened to move from casual play into something that might matter, he'd pulled his usual MO and hit the ground running.

But Jaime Heller had called him on his shit.

She was looking at him now, waiting, he knew, for some kind of response to her ultimatum that he could take what she offered—a chance to really connect in a meaningful way with someone he might truly be able to love—or leave it, and continue as he always had, footloose, fancy free, and alone.

He reached for the hand she'd pulled away, drawing it to him. He lifted her hand to his mouth and lightly kissed her palm.

"I'll take it," he said.

~*~

"You did what?" Annette shouted into Jaime's cell phone.

"I told him I don't want to be a horse whisperer," Jaime repeated. "I told him I don't want to play games—that what we'd shared mattered too much to me."

Jaime was lying on her bed in her studio apartment. As if the gods had conspired against them, Donovan's cell phone had buzzed urgently in his pocket just after he made his earnest pronouncement. He'd been called away on an emergency with the volunteer ambulance corps, though he'd promised to come by the instant he was free.

As the hours had passed, however, Jaime realized they wouldn't be getting together before work. Several apologetic texts from Donovan confirmed this, and Jaime tried to keep her disappointment at bay. After all, they had all the time in the world, right?

"And you're alone now, right?" Annette demanded. "What happened? Did he suddenly make up an excuse and hightail it out of there? Shit, Jaime. Guys like that need to be kept at arm's length for a while. They have to think *they're* the ones who came up with the idea to get together. No offense, girlfriend, but you're a slow study when it comes to snaring a man."

Jaime laughed, shaking her head, though Annette couldn't see her. "You've been a great friend, Annette, and I really appreciate it. You helped me understand what Donovan's issues are and that what he was doing wasn't personal, but I just can't play that kind of girl-tricks-the-guy-into-a-ring game. It's not my style. Either he wants me or he doesn't. I don't want a man I have to trick into being with me."

Annette snorted. "Spoken like a true Domme. Hopefully Donovan manages to get his head out of his ass so he doesn't lose you. Because you're a definite keeper, Mistress Jaime, make no mistake."

Any seeds of doubt Annette had planted during their phone conversation were washed away with Donovan's kiss that night at the club. He came in just a few minutes after Jaime arrived, looking incredibly sexy, as always, in black leather and boots, a lock of his dark hair falling over one eye.

Without preamble and right in front of the new waitress, Suzanne, who was preening in the mirror in the changing room, Donovan had pulled Jaime into his arms. He had kissed her lightly at first, a brushing of his mouth against hers, but after a moment he pressed her lips apart with his tongue, exploring her mouth as his hands moved greedily over her back and ass, pulling her tight against his hard body.

Gene had entered the changing room just seconds after Donovan had let her go. He took in the scene with a knowing smile, though he made no comment. "Jaime, glad you're here. Let's go over the equipment and protocol in the red room one more time. I have a feeling you're going to be very busy tonight."

Once the club opened for the evening, Jaime, dressed to kill in a red leather mini-dress and matching thigh-high red leather boots, had been swarmed by submissives, male and female alike, all eager for a private session. As Gene had predicted, apparently word had gotten out overnight that there was a smoking hot Mistress on the premises, and attendance was at weekend levels though it was only a Wednesday night. Maybe the novelty of it would die off after a week or two, but meanwhile Jaime was having a blast.

Finally she managed a break, having thought to block out the ten to ten-thirty slot so she could watch the Master's first show. She stood toward the back of the room, glad for a moment not to be the center of so much submissive attention. She watched Donovan scan the audience for a potential volunteer.

"Amy," he said, pointing to a woman with long, straight hair whose hand was raised high. "Let's show them what you can do."

Amy was tall, nearly as tall as the Master in her black boots. She was wearing a long black gown with slits cut high along either leg. She was in her twenties and while her makeup was a little heavy and her platinum blond hair probably from a bottle, she was quite striking, especially from a distance.

Jaime felt a sharp pang of jealousy when Donovan took the young woman's hand and led her to center stage. While she didn't dismiss the feeling, she told herself it wasn't necessary. If they were to become lovers and even, someday, partners, she would need to accept his active involvement in the scene, just as he would need to accept hers.

Donovan murmured something inaudible to Amy and then turned to face the crowd. As he spoke, he seemed to be scanning the audience. Jaime, preferring to remain unseen, shrank back in the shadows.

"Tonight," Donovan announced, "you will be treated to watching a true pain slut take a serious caning. For the Doms out there, let me caution you in advance—this is *not* something to try at home, not unless you really know what you're doing, and your sub has a high threshold for pain. Canes can cut the skin, and it's easier to do than you might think."

He turned to Amy, who had unzipped and stepped out of her gown. She stood in a black push-up bra, a black lace thong, and stockings and garters, her boots still in place. Without a trace of self-consciousness she reached behind her back and unclasped her bra, letting it fall to the stage. She stood straight, her heavy breasts tipped with large brown nipples, hands on her hips as she stared down at the crowd gathered around the stage with an enigmatic smile.

"Arms overhead," Donovan instructed. Amy lifted her arms high, standing patiently while Donovan locked them into soft leather cuffs that dangled from ropes that were secured to a pulley over her head. There was play in the rope that allowed Amy to turn, which she now did at Donovan's command, turning until she was facing away from the audience.

Even from where she stood at the back of the room, Jaime could see the faint crisscross of purple and pink lines covering her back, ass and thighs, evidence of prior and repeated whippings with a single tail or a cane. She found herself wondering if Donovan had been one of the Masters to mark her in this fashion, and pushed the thought from her head. If he was, or he wasn't, it didn't matter. No more than it mattered that she'd just whipped, flogged, cuffed, clipped and clamped half a dozen subs in the red room. It was just part of the job, part of the scene.

Donovan selected a long, thin cane, whipping it in the air several times for effect. Amy didn't flinch or make a sound. What she did do was bend forward as far as her wrist cuffs allowed, thrusting her bottom out, a clear invitation for the cane.

The Master began slowly, tapping her ass lightly with the flat of the cane until the skin turned pink. He moved the cane in a rapid, circular motion, the rattan barely touching the skin.

Then a sudden flick of his wrist raised the first welt along her left cheek, a long white line that darkened almost immediately red. The audience offered a collective gasp, though Amy remained still as stone.

Again and again the Master struck her, adding easily a dozen more welts to her ass and thighs, each one expertly placed just above or below the last in neat, horizontal lines.

"More?" the Master asked the bound woman.

"Yes, please, Master! More!" she cried.

"Turn," he instructed, touching Amy's shoulder. She pivoted as gracefully as a dancer, the rope above her wrists winding as she moved. Donovan placed the cane in the rack and selected a shorter, thinner cane. He returned to Amy, murmuring something inaudible to her. She nodded, smiling at him with a look of submissive adoration Jaime knew so well.

Donovan began to tap her breasts, the cane landing skillfully above and below but never directly on the nipples. It wasn't long before he was again painting white lines that quickly reddened as the welts rose on the woman's bare breasts.

Amy was breathing hard now, no longer the perfect picture of calm submission. Jaime could see the sweat sliding down her sides and shining on her forehead. Her large nipples were fully erect, her body trembling ever so slightly.

"Ready?" Donovan asked.

"Yes, please, Master!" Amy shouted, surprising Jaime with the force of her reply.

Donovan paused a beat, taking aim, and let the cane come down directly on Amy's right nipple. Still she didn't cry out, though her face crumpled with pain, her eyes squeezing shut, her lips pressed hard together.

"And again?" Donovan asked, as he moved behind her to her other side.

Once again Amy shouted her agreement, and Donovan flicked the tip of the cane against her other nipple, drawing another anguished expression from the pain slut.

"More?"

"Yes, please, Master! More!"

Donovan turned Amy so her back was again to the audience. Everyone seemed to be holding their breath, including Jaime. The Master flicked the cane against that delicate spot where the ass meets the thighs and then added several more strokes to each thigh.

"More?" he queried.

Again Amy shouted her agreement. Jaime realized she was never going to tell him to stop. Donovan would have to gauge when the girl had had enough.

He turned her again, painting the fronts of her thighs with angry red lines, and adding a few more strokes to her already welted breasts. Amy's entire body glimmered with sweat beneath the stage lights and her face had taken on the glazed, unfocused expression of someone who was soaring through subspace.

Donovan nodded toward the side of the stage and Gene came quickly forward, going to Amy's other side. While he released the cuffs, Donovan caught the girl, who sank, with his help, to her knees. She continued the forward movement until her forehead touched the stage, extending her arms along the stage floor in a classic position of slavish homage to the man who had given her what she longed for, what she craved.

After a moment of hushed silence, the crowd burst into applause. A man, probably Amy's owner, vaulted up to the stage, not even bothering with the stairs. He crouched beside Amy and pulled her gently up into his arms. She looked at him with a dazed expression. She managed to wrap her arms around his neck, allowing him to lift and carry her from the stage while the audience stamped and hooted its approval.

Donovan looked past the crowd, his gaze landing directly on Jaime, though she'd thought he couldn't see her in the shadows. "You're next," he silently mouthed, and then he smiled, a slow, sensuous smile that sent shivers from Jaime's head right down to her toes.

# Chapter 16

As happened each morning since Jaime had been with him, Donovan became aware of her presence before he came fully awake. A kind of mystified wonder suffused his being, a vague but persistent happiness that still startled him with its newness. He felt the curve of her warm body against his and smelled the perfume of her scent. Happiness fanned into a hot, steady fire that radiated from his heart to his loins. His cock hardened, despite the fact they'd made love several times the night before. He pulled her closer, seeking the wet, hot sweetness at her center.

"You must always be ready for me," he'd told her that first night he took her home after their brief separation. "If you are to belong to me, you will always be in a state of constant arousal, ready, eager, even desperate to serve me."

"But—" she started to protest. He'd stopped her with two fingers pressed against her soft lips.

"If you're not wet and aching for my touch, it won't be your fault, darling Jaime." He took his fingers from her lips, staring deep into her sage-green eyes. "It will be mine."

It had been years since Donovan had found someone with whom he connected on so many levels.

He'd always enjoyed playing the scene, selecting a new girl as whim and desire dictated. But this felt different. It felt right. For the first time in his life one woman was enough, as long as that woman was Jaime.

They'd been together for twelve days, though due to their full schedules they hadn't focused as much on Jaime's training as Donovan would have liked. Jaime had spent a few nights at her apartment during the first week, but Donovan had convinced her that her place was at his side, and in his bed. He literally could not get enough of her. She'd only paid rent through the end of the month, and he was hoping to convince her to move in with him at the end of that time, as he was longing to claim her fully, 24/7, 365.

He was looking forward to the two weeks in August when they closed the club. He planned to take Jaime on a vacation to somewhere secluded, where they could fully indulge in their D/s relationship without any distractions.

Jaime and Annette had referred to him as a wild horse, one not easily tamed. Maybe that was true, but so far with Jaime he didn't mind wearing the saddle of a relationship. He felt as wild and free as he ever had. Or he almost did. In his completely honest moments he had to admit there was a little burr beneath the saddle, one he hadn't really been willing to face, hoping it would work its way out on its own.

He didn't really understand his own reaction in this regard, and wondered if maybe it was because he was falling in love with Jaime, something he'd never done before, not ever. Sure, he'd been incredibly fond of and certainly wildly attracted to, various women over the years, but this love thing was new.

The issue was this: he had a hard time watching Mistress Jaime in action. Though he'd never thought of himself as jealous, each time he saw Jaime leading another guy into the red room it was like a knife jabbing into his gut. Intellectually he knew he had no right to feel this way. Jaime was her own woman, strong, confident and independent. Indeed, that was part of his attraction to her. But emotionally it was a whole other ballgame. She was his, damn it, and he'd never been very good at sharing.

He worried there was something even more insidious beneath his possessiveness, but each time he tried to fix on it, it would slip away.

Jaime stirred beside him in the bed, stretching like a sleek cat. Then her head of tousled red hair disappeared as she burrowed beneath the sheets. Donovan sighed with pleasure as his shaft was sheathed in her warm, wet mouth. He surrendered to her sensual touch, his mind emptying as his cock hardened.

When the pleasure was nearly too acute to bear, Donovan gently pushed the suckling girl away from his groin and pulled her up into his arms.

"I wasn't done," she protested, though she was smiling.

"No," Donovan replied with an answering smile. "You're just beginning." He rolled Jaime onto her back and hoisted himself over her. He kissed her forehead and then her eyelids, one at a time. He kissed her nose and then her lips. He kissed her cheeks and her chin before moving down to nuzzle her neck. He kissed the delicate hollow of her throat and then the tops of her breasts. He licked, suckled and then lightly bit her engorged nipples until she moaned.

Finally he shifted downward and crouched between her legs. Jaime was watching him with hungry eyes. "Put your hands over your head," he ordered. "Grasp your wrists and don't let go, no matter what I do to you, understand?"

Jaime nodded, and Donovan's cock hardened even more, if that was possible, as she lifted her arms and grasped each wrist with the opposite hand. She held them aloft for several seconds before letting them fall back to the pillows.

Donovan ran his tongue lightly down her belly, purposely bypassing her cunt as he covered each thigh with butterfly kisses. When she was begging with everything except her words, he finally relented and pressed her thighs apart, the warmth of his breath against her sex making her shiver.

He ran his tongue along the folds of her labia and licked in a teasing circle around her hard little clit. It wasn't long before she was panting and moaning, begging him for permission to come.

"Not yet," he said huskily, now desperate to penetrate her heat. Roughly he pushed her thighs apart with his knee. Grabbing his throbbing cock, he guided the head to her entrance and gently nudged, only barely resisting the powerful urge to plunge into her with one thrust.

Almost the instant he entered her, Jaime began to buck. Her skin was hot, as if she had a fever, and her eyes were wild. "Yes, yes, yes, yes," she began to chant. And then, as he pushed deeper into the tight clutch of her cunt, "Please! Please, please, please, please, oh, can I, oh…!"

"Yes," Donovan managed to hiss, before his orgasm left him deaf, mute and blind.

That Saturday night at the club Gene and Donovan sat side-by-side in Gene's office, their chairs turned toward the glass wall at the back of the room, which was actually a one-way mirror into the red room, where Mistress Jaime was now working with one of her clients.

Gene had chosen the red room for her sessions primarily so Tommy, the bouncer, could spot check to make sure the men she was domming were behaving themselves. So far there hadn't been any problems of that sort, and hopefully there never would be, but Donovan and Annette had agreed it didn't hurt to err on the side of caution.

Donovan was between shows, and while he'd generally tried to stay away from Jaime's turf, sometimes he just couldn't help himself. It was like picking the scab over a fresh wound. He knew he should leave it alone, but it wouldn't leave *him* alone.

"This is working out even better than we thought," Gene enthused, his eyes glued to the scene as they watched Jaime select a heavy flogger from the whip rack. She moved toward a large, bald man in his sixties who was cuffed to a St. Andrew's cross on the far side of the small room. "I knew she would be a popular addition," Gene went on, "but I had no idea it would take off to this degree. The first weekend I thought maybe it was the novelty of it — a flash in the pan — but here we are at weekend two, and she's as popular as ever. Attendance is up overall. We are, my friend," he turned to Donovan with a broad grin, "the latest new thing. Thanks to Mistress Jaime."

"Uh huh." Donovan managed. He tried, but failed to tear his eyes away from the scene in the red room. Jaime leaned over the man to whisper something in his ear. From the way she was standing, her breasts must be pressing against his back.

Stepping back, Jaime began to flog the man, her arm an extension of the whip handle as the thick strands of black leather smacked against his back and ass. The guy's head was tilted back toward the ceiling, his hands opening and closing over his wrist cuffs. Though they couldn't hear much from the other side of the mirror, Donovan bet the bastard was moaning.

"Jesus," Donovan swore under his breath.

Gene glanced sharply at him and then chuckled. "I never thought I'd see the day."

"What?" Donovan demanded, aware he sounded defensive.

"You're jealous. Donovan Cartwright is jealous. Which is pretty rich, given you do the same thing night after night, though, granted, you mostly do it up on the stage."

"Ha!" Donovan retorted. "I respect Jaime's right to practice her craft, same as I do. What makes you think I'm jealous?"

"I've known you for a long time, my friend. The green-eyed monster is glowing from your eyes every time you look through that mirror." Gene patted Donovan's shoulder affectionately. "Hey, your secret's safe with me. It's okay to be a little jealous, as long as you don't let it control you. It means you care."

Donovan regarded Gene, both relieved and annoyed to have been called out on his feelings, feelings he hadn't shared with Jaime because he knew they were unfair. "It's hard," he admitted finally. "Hard to watch her with those other guys."

Gene nodded. "I know. You Dom types are especially jealous. I guess it comes with the territory." He shrugged. "Why do you think I never scene at the club? Annette would tear me a new one. You think you're possessive!" He laughed, placing his hand over his crotch. Donovan knew he wore a leather chastity belt while out of the house, as a constant reminder of Annette's ownership. He also knew that Gene had been the one to petition for the device.

Donovan lifted his chin in acknowledgment of Gene's words, aware of the deep love between Annette and Gene. Annette's total control of all aspects of Gene's life worked between them, but would it work between Jaime and him? Would he want Jaime in a chastity belt, forbidden to scene, except with him? His head answered with a staunch *no*! But his heart wasn't so sure. But was it his heart, or something else at play?

The client was dressing, the scene apparently over. Once she was alone, Jaime moved toward the mirror, examining her face and reapplying her lipstick as if she didn't remember there might be people watching her on the other side. She looked spectacular in her black velvet vest and skirt, her breasts bunched alluringly together to create a deep cleavage, the slits in the skirt revealing her long legs.

Donovan's cock twitched with desire and his heart fairly ached with longing.

A moment later Jaime turned back to the door, probably in response to a knock they couldn't hear, and then moved toward it, opening it to a young man Donovan hadn't seen around the club before. He was tall and way too good looking, with a head of thick blond hair and a chiseled jaw. He was dressed in a business suit, of all things, his expensive-looking tie loosened around his neck.

"Oh I remember this guy's session card," Gene said eagerly. "He's some kind of high powered business dude by day, total pain slut by night. Looks like he stepped right out of GQ, huh?" Donovan made no reply as he stared through the mirror. Jaime had picked up the session card, which contained the details of what the client wanted, and was reading it. Gene had come up with the idea of creating the cards in advance when he took payment, so Mistress Jaime could focus on the scene without having to tease the client's fantasy out of them.

Jaime moved to the supply cabinet while the man was stripping. The guy's physique was an upside down triangle, his broad shoulders narrowing to the point of his slender waist and hips. His lines were long and lean, his body hairless, his dick, even while semi-flaccid, porn-star huge.

Donovan realized his hands had curled into fists at his sides, and a part of him would have loved to smash one of them right across that square jaw and then into those six-pack abs. *Cool it,* he told himself, trying to calm down. *This is not sexual. Jaime belongs to you. That's not even Jaime behind the mirror, it's Mistress Jaime.* It didn't work. Donovan bounced lightly on the balls of his feet, his eyes burning through the glass.

Mr. GQ extended his arms and stood patiently while Jaime cuffed his wrists to the chains hanging overhead. Jaime attached clothespins in a ring around each of the man's nipples. She added more pins to his denuded balls, catching the loose skin of his scrotum in a fan of clothespins. Mr. GQ winced in pain each time she attached another pin, but his cock elongated to an obscene length, and was dripping with pre-come by the time she was done.

Jaime selected a single tail from the rack and began to expertly flick the clothespins from the man's chest, one by one. Each time the whip met its mark and a clothespin flew, the man mouthed the words, "Thank you, Mistress," while flinching in pain.

When all the clothespins had been flicked from his chest, his nipples were ringed with angry red splotches. The man was panting, his eyes scrunched shut, his chest heaving. Jaime's back was to the mirror, but she must have said something, because the man opened his eyes and took a deep breath.

He nodded, now mouthing the words, "Yes, Mistress. Please, Mistress."

Positioning herself, Jaime flicked the whip toward the man's scrotum and one of the pins flew to the ground. The man's mouth opened in an O of agony, but his cock remained hard as steel. The whip struck again, and again, each time hitting its target dead on.

All at once a flush of color washed over the man's neck, his tongue suddenly snaking over his lips as his eyes flew open. It took Donovan a moment to realize what he was seeing. As the tethered man stared with wild eyes at Jaime, he began to shudder and his cock erupted in a stream of ejaculate.

"God damn it!" Donovan roared, turning abruptly from the scene.

"Donovan!" Gene hissed. "Keep your voice down. They heard you."

"I don't care. Pull a curtain on that fucking thing. I can't stand it." He strode from the office, fury propelling him, though he had no idea where he was going. He found himself heading toward the back exit. He shoved the door open with his shoulder and stepped out into the cool, foggy night. He slammed himself against the wall of the building and hit the back of his head against the bricks again and again, glad for the distraction of the pain.

After a moment the door of the building opened, and Gene came out to stand beside him. Donovan was breathing hard and adrenaline was skittering through his blood, as if he'd just been in a fight. Neither of them spoke for a long moment. Donovan drew in a deep breath as he tried to clear his head and slow his thudding heart. He knew he was being a jerk. He just didn't know how to stop.

"I remember what it felt like," Gene began softly, his eyes straight ahead, "when I used to go to Madame Anika." That, Donovan knew, had been Annette's professional name when she had worked as a pro Domme. "When I first started in the scene," Gene continued, "I didn't really know what I wanted. Or no, correct that. I knew what I wanted, but I had a very hard time admitting my submissive and masochistic needs. I worked in construction, for god's sake. I grew up in a house with three brothers and a father who taught us from an early age that real men didn't cry. Real men had no emotions of any sort, when it came down to it, except maybe rage and righteous anger. And women were made for two things—to make babies and clean the kitchen. Definitely *not* to serve and worship."

The pain in Gene's voice shocked Donovan out of his own narcissistic funk. He knew Gene's early history in a vague sort of way, but this was the first time Gene had spilled his guts like this. Donovan put his hand gently on his old friend's shoulder. Gene continued to stare straight ahead, but he didn't stop talking.

"Ever since I was sexually aware, I knew I had different feelings inside. Unacceptable feelings. *Dirty* feelings. It took me years to get up the courage to even begin to explore them. I'd visited other Dommes before Annette, but they'd always treated me in a way that confirmed my own secret shame. They would call me names, like sniveling worm, or worthless piece of shit, and one even spit on me." He sighed and then continued, "Madame Anika was different. She was a tough taskmaster, make no mistake, but she treated me with respect. She understood my masochistic needs and longing to submit, without making me feel *less than*, if you follow me."

He turned at last to Donovan and smiled. "I fell in love with her the very first session, though at the time I was too fucking clueless to realize it. I nearly bankrupted myself that first year booking sessions with her." He laughed ruefully. "But it was never going to work, you see?" He shook his head with a snort.

"She was a pro and I was just a client, right?" he asked rhetorically, though he didn't pause long enough for Donovan to answer, even if he'd wanted to. "But as time went on, something started to change between us. We didn't just scene. She would talk to me afterwards, sometimes for an hour or longer. A real connection was developing between us, but I was terrified to do anything about it, because I kept rationalizing why she would want to hang out with me—she felt sorry for such a loser, she was really bored that day, anything to avoid confronting my own feelings. I kept my mouth shut about how I really felt for a long time. I wasn't willing to risk the humiliation. I wasn't willing to be vulnerable in front of her. I wasn't willing to trust her."

He paused for a long time before finally continuing. "Annette continued to be a pro Domme for a few years into our relationship, you know. And yeah, I'll admit sometimes it was hard for me to know what she was doing to some other guy. It took me a while to really accept it wasn't about sex, and it sure as hell wasn't about love." He turned at last to look Donovan in the eye. "Annette and I have been together for a long time. There is no way we would have lasted this long, no matter how much we loved each other, without the most essential thing of any relationship. It's the bedrock of BDSM, and it's also the bedrock of love. You know what I'm talking about, Donovan, I know you do. You're too good at what you do not to know it. And once you find it, once you share it with another person, you can surmount any odds."

Donovan stared at Gene, the tension and anger suddenly draining from his body as if a plug had been pulled. In its place a curious, rising joy was pushing its way into his consciousness. All at once he knew what Gene was saying. He understood it, deep in his bones, beyond the level of thought or words. It was the missing piece of the puzzle, the thing he'd never really shared in an intimate relationship, the thing that had enabled him to keep others at arm's length, the thing that had kept him alone. The thing he wanted suddenly with Jaime, more than he'd ever wanted anything before.

"Trust," he whispered.

Gene laughed, nodding. "You got it. It's a matter of trust."

# Chapter 17

Jaime lay in the bed, drifting in that space between consciousness and dreams. She could feel Donovan's warm, solid presence beside her and hear the soft rumble of his quiet snore.

Opening her eyes, Jaime glanced at the clock beside the bed. It was only nine o'clock on Sunday morning—they had the whole glorious weekend to themselves. She rolled toward Donovan, examining the sleeping man in the gold wash of early light filling the room. She examined the lines and planes of his face and watched the soft rise and fall of his chest. It was too early to wake him, even by kissing his cock, her favorite way to rouse the Master.

As they were drifting off to sleep the night before, or technically earlier that morning, Donovan had held her face in his hands, gazing at her with a solemn, almost fierce gaze. The moon shone through the window, casting the room in a shimmery, ephemeral light. "It's going to be different now, Jaime," he said softly, his voice cracking with emotion. "I promise."

She hadn't understood him, at least not with her head. Yet when he spoke those words, a tightness she didn't realize had been constricting her heart eased and softened.

Aloud, she'd asked, *"What's* going to be different?"

He had answered with a kiss. It hadn't been like the teasing, playful kisses they shared over breakfast or while stopped at a traffic light, or the intense, claiming kiss of the Master, but something different, something achingly tender and sweet. She had fallen asleep with the imprint of that kiss on her lips.

Now she touched the snakes coiling around his biceps, tracing the bright triangles of color along their scaly backs with her finger. She became aware Donovan was awake, his blue eyes tracking the movement of her finger along his biceps.

"Morning, sexy," he said sleepily.

"Morning to you. I hope I didn't wake you."

"Nah, I've been drifting in and out for a while now."

He reached for her, but before she fell into his arms, Jaime said, "I keep meaning to ask what's behind this tattoo." She grinned. "But somehow you keep distracting me before I can find out."

Donovan smiled. "Well, I could tell you I got shitfaced drunk one night and when I woke up, there it was."

Jaime lifted her eyebrows, examining his face to see if he was joking. He laughed, shaking his head.

"Actually, if you knew me back in my early twenties, that definitely would have been a possibility. But no," he shook his head at her unasked question, "luckily I never did anything that dumb, or at least nothing that left any permanent evidence."

"So…?" Jaime prompted, her curiosity piqued.

Donovan hoisted himself onto an elbow as he turned to face her. "A really cool tattoo artist did that for me, a Domme, as a matter of fact, who I met when I was first getting really involved in the scene in my mid-twenties. She was always talking about the trinities of BDSM, as she referred to it. Everything, she said, came in threes."

This time when he reached again for her, Jaime allowed herself to be pulled into Donovan's arms. As she snuggled against his chest, he continued. "She said you have the three divisions of BDSM—B&D, D/s and S&M, and then you have the three-way core tenets of *safe, sane and consensual*, and then you have the divisions common in the community—Top or Dom, sub or bottom, and switch.

"She wanted to give me the traditional BDSM emblem, you know the one, it looks sort of like a ying-yang symbol, except there are three sections?" When Jaime nodded, Donovan continued, "Well, I didn't want that. I've always been fascinated with snakes, which are symbols of rebirth and transformation in a lot of mythology. So I thought, why not combine the two concepts? And"—he touched the snakes on his upper arm—"that's what she did."

"I want a tattoo," Jaime said, suddenly excited by the idea.

Donovan laughed. "Eventually, maybe. Once you'd had plenty of time to get used the idea. Tattoos are definitely *not* something you do on the spur of the moment."

Untangling himself gently from her embrace, Donovan rolled from the bed. Leaning over her, he pulled the sheets from Jaime and ran his hand proprietarily over her bare body, his eyes hooding with lust. "Let's take a shower."

Jaime followed him into the bathroom. They both used the toilet and brushed their teeth with as much ease and familiarity as if they'd been together for years, instead of just the few weeks it actually had been. Their eyes met in the mirror as they set their toothbrushes down and Jaime saw the sudden spark of masterful fire in Donovan's gaze and felt her own answering rush of hot, submissive desire.

He led her to the large shower stall and pulled open the glass door, stepping in first to adjust the temperature. When he'd got it just right, he beckoned for her to enter and Jaime joined him, pulling the glass door closed behind her.

The water felt wonderful, hot and steamy, and Jaime let it sluice over her head and body for a moment before reaching for the soap. In the several times they'd showered together a pattern had been established. Jaime would wash Donovan's body, spending extra time on his cock and balls until he would pull her up into his arms.

This time however, Donovan stopped her hand with his. "This morning I will wash you. Today is for you, slave girl. All for you."

*Slave girl.*

Of course, she wasn't actually his slave girl. Theirs was a consensual and continually negotiated erotic dance between Dom and sub, rather than a Master/slave relationship where the slave, albeit willingly, gave up all semblance of decision or control. Nevertheless, when he called her that, when he said the words *slave girl*, the submissive embers banked at the core of Jaime's being burst into flame, and a small *oh* of pure thrill was pulled from her lips.

Donovan took the bar of soap and rubbed it in his hands, creating a thick, creamy lather. He moved his hands sensually over her skin, his touch sending shivery jolts of electricity through her muscle and bone. He squirted shampoo into the palm of his hand and washed her hair, massaging her scalp with his strong fingers. He had her lean her head back while he rinsed her hair and then pulled conditioner through, before rinsing it, too, beneath the hot rush of water.

"Hands over head, legs apart," Donovan instructed. Jaime lifted her arms high and clasped her hands together over her head, her heart thudding in her chest. He picked up her pink razor. "Stay still. I'm going to groom you." With his skillful, careful touch he shaved her underarms. Crouching in front of her, he smoothed baby oil over her calves and stroked the razor along her skin. Standing with her arms high over her head, her lover kneeling before her, even this potentially mundane task took on an erotically charged aspect.

Finally he had her sit on the tile-covered bench at the back of the stall, her legs spread wide, her cunt exposed to the sharp multi-bladed razor. Jaime closed her eyes, a frisson of fear shivering its way through her body, even though she trusted Donovan completely and implicitly. He stroked her with the blades, the tips of his fingers following in their wake. He set aside the razor but his fingers remained, gliding over her labia.

He lifted the removable showerhead from its base and pointed it directly at her spread cunt. Even after all the soap was washed away, he kept the pulsing water aimed at her, adjusting the spray to a fine, directed point.

"Hold your cunt open for me," he ordered. "Push yourself out to meet the spray." Jaime obeyed, closing her eyes against the onslaught of hot water pummeling her clit. Already extremely aroused by the washing and grooming, it wasn't long before Jaime approached orgasm.

"Come for me," Donovan ordered, at just the right moment that made it easy to obey. Jaime let herself go, shuddering and gasping as the spray pulsed steadily against her spasming sex. Her hands started to slip as she came. "Hold your position," Donovan said sternly. "I didn't give you permission to let go of your cunt."

A second orgasm rolled over the first as Jaime struggled to hold herself open to the intense, continual stimulation of the streaming water. "Oh god!" she cried, as yet a third climax crashed through her. "Help me!"

Donovan chuckled softly, but mercifully he replaced the shower head in its slot overhead. He pulled Jaime gently from the bench, but instead of allowing her to rise, he pressed her to her knees. His erect cock brushed her cheek and she needed no further instruction.

As the hot water rained down on her back and shoulders and steam swirled around them, Jaime took Donovan's cock deep in her throat. She cradled his heavy balls in her hands as she bobbed over his groin, worshipping his cock with every ounce of her being.

When he ejaculated deep in her throat, she barely had to swallow. Not ready to let him go, she continued to suck and stroke his shaft with her mouth, lips and tongue. She felt as if she could do this forever. She was completely consumed with her delicious task. It wasn't about power or control, as it had been with the other men in her life, but rather about giving over, about surrendering to the pure, raw masculinity of this perfect man who stood before her. She would have kissed and suckled him for as long as he let her. But he was pulling back, his hands lightly on her shoulders as he stepped away. Reaching for her, he drew her up into his arms.

When they got out of the shower she picked up a towel, suddenly feeling the need to serve the Master. She was silently grateful when he permitted her to do this small but centering task. She ran the terrycloth carefully over his naked body and limbs, adding a kiss to the head of his penis when she was done, which made him laugh, and she laughed too, beyond happy.

She knelt on the cushion in the kitchen while she watched Donovan prepare a simple breakfast of toast and fresh peaches with cream, along with strong, hot coffee. He fed her lovingly, and each bite was more delicious than the last.

When they'd both had their fill, he did a very curious thing. Taking her left hand in his, he stroked her ring finger with the tips of his thumb and forefinger, as if he were placing an invisible ring there. She met his gaze, a question in her eyes. He smiled and said enigmatically, "Trust. A matter of trust."

~*~

Donovan led Jaime into the playroom and had her stand on the mat in the center of the room. "Hands overhead," he instructed, excited at the scene he had planned for her. Ever since the epiphany he'd experienced in the parking lot with Gene the night before, Donovan had felt different. Lighter, somehow, as if heavy chains he hadn't even realized he'd been dragging along behind him had suddenly been cut away.

The very thing he asked, or in truth, demanded of his subs was the very thing he had withheld from Jaime. Listening to Gene, he had understood suddenly that his anger when he watched Mistress Jaime with her sub boys wasn't about concern for her safety or even jealousy that she might fall for another guy.

Beneath the anger was fear. A fear he would have staunchly denied if Gene hadn't somehow penetrated the armor of his denial with one well-placed stroke. Why was it he'd never found a woman to love? Why was it, at age thirty-two, he was still alone at the end of the day, never satisfied with what he had, always finding fault or lack in whoever he was with, and in so doing absolving himself of any responsibility for his failure to connect?

It was about trust!

Trust not only in the woman he was with, but in himself. Trust that he had what it took to enter into and sustain a mature, loving relationship with another person. Trust that he had the courage to be vulnerable with the one person who had the power to hurt him the most.

He didn't want to stop Jaime from being who she was, any more than he would have wanted to stop being Master in residence at the club just because he'd met the girl of his dreams. He loved Jaime, he understood now, not in spite of her dominant side, but *because* of it, because of precisely and exactly who she was, as complex and fascinating as any woman he'd ever known. By example she had shown him what true courage was, the courage to submit when it was scary, the courage to be vulnerable in the face of uncertainty.

And by example, she had taught him what trust was about. She had given him no reason to doubt her, not once, not for a second. No matter how many men crowded around her, or how intense the scenes she executed in the red room became, Jaime always and only had eyes for him, for her Master, for Donovan.

He wrapped the Velcro cuffs around Jaime's wrists and attached them to the chains hanging from the ceiling beam. Going to the wall, he turned the winch to raise the chains until Jaime's arms were taut overhead, her luscious breasts lifted like an offering.

He moved to stand in front of her, his cock tenting his boxer shorts at the sight of the lovely young woman in his chains, utterly at his mercy. He tugged the underwear down his legs and kicked it away.

He leaned down and kissed her mouth, slowly, lingeringly, while letting his hands roam over her smooth, bare body. He rolled her nipples in his fingers until they were hard beneath the spongy flesh. He let his hand trail down between her legs, slipping a finger into her wetness and grinding his palm against her spread sex until she groaned.

Finally letting her go, he stepped back so he could look deep into her eyes. "Do you trust me, slave girl?"

"Yes, Sir," she breathed, her eyes fluttering shut.

"Open your eyes," he instructed. "Look at me." He waited while she obeyed. Keeping his gaze locked on hers, he said, "Today I'm going to take you further than we've been before. I'm going to test that trust." He reached for her throat, stroking the supple skin with his thumb and forefinger. She shuddered and her lips parted, her reaction zinging directly to Donovan's cock.

"I'm going to control your breath," he informed her, tightening his grip slightly on her throat. "You will keep your eyes open and your gaze on mine. I will count, letting you know beforehand how long we'll go. Okay?"

"Yes, Sir," she said again. She had begun to tremble, but he could sense the steel of her resolve beneath the fear.

"Ten seconds to start," he informed her. He moved his hand upward along her slender neck, stopping when his thumb and forefinger lodged firmly beneath her jaw on either side. He pressed hard and she drew in a sudden, sharp breath. He pressed harder still, aware now she could no longer breathe.

"Ten," he began. "Nine, eight, seven…"

When he let her go, he slapped her cheek, a sudden, sharp smack that made her gasp and jerk her head back. Her eyes were glittering, her breathing ragged. When he put his hand between her legs, she was sopping wet.

Donovan felt himself slipping fully into Dom mode, the knowledge of his position and her reactions more powerful than any drug. He felt like a god, capable of anything, the world at his command. At the same time, he was keenly aware of the responsibility that went along with the power. It was like holding a precious jewel in his hands. He made a silent promise to keep his jewel safe and happy, while still giving her the submissive experience she craved.

"Fifteen," he announced, again catching her throat with his big hand and squeezing. As he counted down this time, Jaime's eyes started to roll back, and he interrupted his count to admonish, "Stay with me! We're only just beginning."

She complied, her focus returning to his face, her eyes locked on his. Again when he released her, he slapped her face, hard, and again she gasped and shuddered, her head jerking back.

"Twenty-five," he intoned. He watched her carefully as he counted backwards. Her face reddened, her hands clenched at the chains. He held fast, certain she could get through this, his cock aching as he held his sub girl's very life in his hands. Her eyes began to roll back and still he didn't let go, though he didn't call her to task, not wanting to stop the count. Her head fell back during the final several seconds, her hands going suddenly limp.

He let her go, once again slapping her cheek to revive her. This time she barely responded, her head still back. Moving closer, Donovan lifted her head. Her eyes were closed but she was breathing. It was not the panicked pant of someone in distress, but the slow, deep breathing of someone in an altered state.

She was flying.

Donovan placed his arms beneath Jaime's ass and lifted her to his waist. "Jaime, darling. Are you okay?"

Without opening her eyes she nodded, a ghost of a smile moving over her lips. Holding her in position,

Donovan grabbed his cock with his other hand and guided its gooey tip to her cunt. She was ready for him, deliciously hot and wet, but he moved carefully, lifting her hips as he guided her onto his rock-hard shaft.

Though her head continued to loll and her eyes remained closed, her body reacted to his invasion, her cunt clamping hard on his cock, her nipples pointing with rosy-red perkiness in his direction. Donovan groaned, aware he was going to come within a few strokes. He thrust forward and back with his pelvis, while continuing to lift and lower her on his shaft.

"Jaime," he groaned, the words torn from him as he began to come. "I love you."

She began to shudder against him, a series of mini-climaxes that milked his cock, drawing every last bit of his seed from him. They stood like that, Jaime still impaled on Donovan's cock, for several long moments afterward, until he came enough to himself to move.

Holding her, he eased his cock from the sweet stickiness of her cunt and set her gently on her feet. Reaching up, he quickly released her cuffs and caught her as she began to sink to the ground. He carried her to the couch and sat down with her still in his arms. She opened her eyes slowly and looked into his eyes, an impish smile lifting the corners of her mouth.

"You do, huh?"

It was the first time he'd said it to her. The first time either of them had said it, in fact. Indeed, he realized with something approaching shock, it was the first time he'd ever said it to anyone.

She tilted her head to regard him, her green eyes dancing as she waited for him to answer.

"Yeah," he said, smiling back. "I do."

~*~

They sat across the small table in a secluded corner of the dining room in celebration of their six month anniversary. Jaime felt sexy in her slinky red dress and matching heels. Donovan looked spectacular in a dark brown sport jacket over a pale blue cashmere sweater that accentuated the vivid blue of his eyes.

Their relationship, they'd agreed, had started the day she had arrived at his house, scared but determined to go through with the forty-eight hours that would change her life forever. Since then their lives had settled into a routine, though it was anything but dull.

They both continued to work by night at the club, and far from being a flash in the pan, Jaime had become well-established as the Mistress in residence, sharing the stage with the Master from time to time, though her focus remained on private sessions in the red room. She loved every minute of it, and her bank account loved it too. She was earning more than double what she'd earned as a loan officer, and having way more fun in the process.

At home they continued their exploration of an increasingly intense and committed D/s relationship, each day more powerful and passionate than the day before. Jaime knew there was nothing she would not do for this man she loved with all her heart. She embraced each new erotic challenge with as much courage as she possessed. Along with the thrilling bondage, whippings and breath play, Donovan had pierced her nipples and her labia, and they were discussing a tattoo or possibly even a brand she would take as his permanent mark of ownership. Jaime was eager to proceed, but Donovan wanted her to wait until she was absolutely sure.

Donovan had shared what he called his epiphany in the parking lot, but even if he hadn't told her, Jaime had sensed the seismic shift between them after that night. The wild horse had bolted for good, leaving in its place a mature and loving man who cherished her not only for her submission, but for her strength. And Jaime, in turn, had learned to trust the Master not only with her body, but with her heart and soul as well.

Tonight everything was perfect—the red wine, the candles, the thick white table cloth, the tinkling of the jazz piano in the corner of the restaurant, and, most importantly, the sexy, handsome man sitting just across from her, grinning like a Cheshire cat.

"Okay," she finally said, after the appetizers had been cleared and their wine glasses refilled. "You look like the cat that ate the canary. What's going on?"

"Man, am I that obvious?" Donovan looked pained, but then he grinned. He reached into the inner pocket of his jacket and pulled out a long, narrow white box wrapped in a blue satin ribbon. He pushed it across the table in Jaime's direction.

She looked up at him, her heart twisting with joy in her chest.

"Go on," he urged. "Open it."

She tugged at the ribbon and it fell away. Lifting the lid of the box she saw a red velvet choker with a gold ring at its center resting in a bed of black satin. "Oh," she said softly, lifting the choker into her hands.

"It's a collar," Donovan said. "Will you wear it for me?"

Jaime nodded, her eyes suddenly filling with tears. Donovan pushed back from his chair and moved to stand behind her. She bowed her head as he took the collar and placed it around her neck, slipping the clasp into place. Instead of returning to his seat, as she'd expected, he knelt beside her.

"There's something else in the box," he said. "Underneath the liner."

Jaime reached for the box, pushing her fingers beneath the satin. They closed over a ring and she pulled it out. It was a simple gold band with a lustrous diamond sparkling at its center.

"There's an inscription," Donovan said, his tone eager and boyish. "Hold it to the candle and see."

Jaime did as instructed, reading the words, "*I am my beloved's, and my beloved is mine.*" She turned to Donovan, speechless. He took the ring gently from her fingers and, still kneeling beside her, took her left hand in his.

He held the ring poised at her fingertip. "Jaime, my slave girl, my beloved," he said, grinning broadly, though she could see the nervousness in his eyes. "Will you marry me?"

She stared at him, the joy in her heart erupting into a happy laugh. "Donovan, Master of my heart, my beloved, yes!"

## Also Available at Romance Unbound Publishing

## (http://romanceunbound.com)

A Lover's Call
A Princely Gift
Accidental Slave
Alternative Treatment
Binding Discoveries
Blind Faith
Cast a Lover's Spell
Caught: Punished by Her Boss
Closely Held Secrets
Club de Sade
Confessions of a Submissive
Continuum of Desire
Dare to Dominate
Dream Master
Face of Submission
Finding Chandler
Frog
Golden Angel
Golden Boy
Heart of Submission
Heart Thief
Island of Temptation
Jewel Thief

Julie's Submission
Lara's Submission
Masked Submission
Obsession: Girl Abducted
Odd Man Out
Perfect Cover
Pleasure Planet
Princess
Safe in Her Arms
Sarah's Awakening
Seduction of Colette
Slave Academy
Slave Castle
Slave Gamble
Slave Girl
Slave Island
Slave Jade
Sold into Slavery
Sub for Hire
Submission Times Two
Switch
Texas Surrender
The Auction
The Compound
The Cowboy Poet
The Solitary Knights of Pelham Bay
The Story of Owen
The Toy
Tough Boy

Tracy in Chains
True Kin Vampire Tales:
   Sacred Circle
   Outcast
   Sacred Blood
True Submission
Two Loves for Alex
Two Masters for Alex
Wicked Hearts

# *Connect with Claire*

Website: http://clairethompson.net

Romance Unbound Publishing: http://romanceunbound.com

Twitter: http://twitter.com/CThompsonAuthor

Facebook: http://www.facebook.com/ClaireThompsonauthor

Made in the USA
San Bernardino, CA
18 September 2017